Threads of Fate: Pieces of Us
By Evelyn Cross

For those who have ever looked back on the fragments of their lives and found beauty in the pieces.
And for anyone who has loved, lost, and dared to love again.

"We are made of moments, some fleeting, some etched into our souls forever. It is in these moments that we find who we truly are."
— Anonymous

To the people who taught me that love is never simple but always worth exploring. To my readers, who bring these stories to life. And to the Cross family, for your unwavering support. You have my endless gratitude.

Life has a way of weaving its threads in unexpected patterns. Some threads shine with joy and laughter; others are frayed with pain and loss. But every thread has a purpose, shaping the fabric of who we are.

This is the story of Ethan and Grace—two people bound by a connection so deep that it survived years of silence, heartbreak, and the choices that pulled them apart. It's a story about the pieces of life that make us whole, even when they leave us longing for what might have been.

As you turn these pages, I invite you to step into their world, to feel their joys and sorrows, and perhaps, to find pieces of yourself within their journey.

Chapter One

The gravel crunched under the tires as Ethan pulled the rental car into the driveway of the house he swore he'd never see again. The engine hummed softly, its sound almost too modern, too polished, for a place that still smelled of rust and damp earth. He killed the ignition and sat back, staring at the peeling paint on the porch steps and the broken window on the left—the one his father had never bothered to fix.

The air felt heavier here, as though the years he'd been gone hadn't thinned the memories that clung to the place. His stomach churned, a mix of regret and resentment swirling inside him. He wasn't here by choice; he'd spent the better part of two weeks ignoring the lawyer's calls before finally caving. *The estate is yours to manage,* the man had said, his voice devoid of sympathy. *Someone has to deal with it.*

And so here he was, staring at the ghost of a childhood he'd spent every waking moment trying to escape.

Ethan opened the car door, stepping out into the crisp late-autumn air. A sharp wind cut through his coat, carrying the faint smell of burning leaves and the promise of an early winter. He shoved his hands into his pockets, trying to brace himself against more than just the cold.

The house hadn't changed much in the decade since he'd left. The shutters still hung lopsided, the gutters sagged under years of neglect, and the yard was an overgrown tangle of weeds. A cracked mailbox leaned precariously by the curb, the name "Blackwell" barely legible beneath layers of dirt and faded memories.

It's just a house, he told himself, but the lump in his throat begged to differ.

As he reached the porch, the creak of wood under his boots pulled his focus to the door. His hand hesitated on the doorknob. He could still remember the sound of it slamming shut, the echo of his father's drunken rage bouncing off these same walls. The thought made his chest tighten

Ethan stepped into the house, the air inside cool and still, as though the walls had swallowed any sign of life that once inhabited them. The familiar creak of the wooden floors underfoot was like a nostalgic ache, reminding him of the way he used to tiptoe across them at night, trying to avoid waking his father after another of his drunken rages.

He paused in the entryway, trying to make sense of the feeling that hit him. The house was still the same—barely changed, despite all the years that had passed. The faint scent of dust hung in the air, mingling with the scent of old wood and fading memories. His father's presence lingered, but it felt distant, as if the house had been waiting for him to return and reclaim it.

Before he could fully take it in, he heard the door behind him creak open. He turned, his gaze falling on Grace as she stepped in from the front porch, just as unexpectedly as if she had been summoned by the very house itself.

Her eyes met his, and for a moment, everything around them seemed to fade away. The years between them vanished as if they had never existed. There she was, standing in the doorway, looking as if time had softened her edges but hadn't changed her at all.

Grace wasn't supposed to be here. Ethan wasn't sure what he had expected, but it certainly wasn't this.

"I... didn't think I'd find you here," he said, his voice hoarse with surprise, still trying to make sense of the moment. "What are you doing here, Grace?"

She gave a small shrug, her hands tucked into the pockets of her jacket, as though she hadn't quite figured out how to stand in front of him after so many years. "I wasn't sure when you'd be back. I didn't think it'd be today, but... well, I guess fate works in strange ways."

Ethan's brow furrowed, confused. "Fate?"

Grace met his gaze, and for a fleeting moment, it was as if she could see all the unsaid words and unfinished stories between them. She smiled, but it was bittersweet, like a memory neither of them could fully hold onto. "I figured you'd need someone here. Just in case. I wasn't sure when you'd show up... but it looks like today's the day."

Ethan's heart stuttered in his chest, the weight of the past crashing into him. "I didn't think anyone would be here."

"Not many people are," she said quietly, stepping farther into the room. "But I didn't want you to face all this alone, not after everything."

Ethan had no idea how to respond. Grace had always been like this—showing up, quietly offering her support without asking for anything in return. She had been his anchor back then, but he had run away, left without so much as a goodbye. And now here she was, standing in front of him, as if no time had passed.

The house felt too small, the air too thick. He didn't know if he was supposed to feel relieved to see her, or if her presence made everything worse, like a reminder of all that had been lost.

"I didn't come here for this," Ethan finally said, swallowing his emotions down. He could feel the tension building in his chest, but he didn't know how to let it out. "I came back to handle things. The estate, the house... everything."

Grace nodded slowly, her eyes soft. "I know. But sometimes fate has a way of putting people exactly where they need to be."

Ethan felt the weight of her words, but they didn't make anything clearer. They just left him with more questions—questions about what had happened to the person he used to be, and whether he could ever become someone different.

Chapter Two

The house was always loud. It was never the kind of loud that came from a family's usual chatter or the sound of happy feet running through the hallways. No, this was a different kind of loud. The kind that gnawed at the edges of the air, a tension so thick it hung over everything like a storm cloud waiting to burst.

Ethan sat quietly on the edge of the couch, knees pulled up to his chest, his blanket wrapped tightly around him like a shield. The television played in the background, but the volume was too low to cut through the sounds from the other room.

"Lila!" Jim's voice came from the kitchen, sharp and cutting through the air. "Where the hell's my dinner?"

Ethan winced, his small body tensing at the sound. It was the same every night. His mother's soft voice tried to calm his father down, to reason with him, but it never worked. Nothing ever worked.

"You know what time it is, Jim," Lila's voice was quiet but firm. "The dinner's almost ready. Just give it a minute."

But Ethan knew his father didn't care about patience. Jim was always impatient. Always angry.

Ethan shifted on the couch, eyes flicking to the kitchen door, where muffled voices grew louder. He could hear the scrape of something heavy being knocked over, a crash. His heart began to race as he pulled the blanket tighter around himself, wishing he could disappear into it.

"Goddamn it, Lila, don't tell me what to do!" Jim's shout echoed, and the sound of a door slamming against the frame made the hairs on the back of Ethan's neck stand up.

There was no comfort in the house, only the deep, gnawing feeling of fear that never quite left him. He tried to block it out, to ignore the growing tension in the air, but it was impossible. It was always there, lurking in the shadows.

"Ethan," his mother's voice reached him, soft but strained. "Don't worry, baby. Everything's going to be okay."

But Ethan knew it wasn't. He could feel it in the way his mother spoke, the way her voice trembled ever so slightly. The storm inside their home was never over. It was only ever waiting to come back.

The door creaked open, and Ethan looked up, his breath catching. His mother stood in the doorway of the living room, her face pale, her hands trembling. She didn't say a word as she set the dinner down on the table, the plate clinking lightly as she placed it. She then turned and knelt beside him, a brief smile that didn't quite reach her eyes.

"Ethan," she whispered, pulling him into her arms. "Everything's going to be okay."

But Ethan couldn't believe her anymore. Not fully. There was no way she could protect him from the storm that always followed his father's anger. All he could do was stay there, in the quiet for as long as it would last.

His mother's arms were the only comfort he had. And in that moment, he didn't want to think about the broken things, the shattered moments that would come after. All he wanted was to be somewhere safe. Somewhere far from the noise and the chaos.

But Ethan knew better. He knew that peace would never last. Not in this house. Not with Jim out there.

The faint smell of burnt food lingered in the air, cutting through the scent of stale beer and something else—something darker. Ethan's eyes darted to the kitchen door again, his heart thudding in his chest, every nerve on edge. He knew what was coming.

Jim's voice boomed from the kitchen, now slurring, thick with anger and alcohol. "You think I'm stupid, Lila? You think I can't smell the bullshit?" His voice cracked, a mix of fury and frustration that spiraled like a tornado, threatening to tear apart whatever semblance of peace the house had left.

Ethan's grip on the blanket tightened, his knuckles white. He knew better than to try and escape to his room—his father would just drag him back, yelling, hitting, breaking anything in his path. So, he stayed there on the couch, his small body shrinking as much as he could, as though becoming smaller would make the storm pass him by.

Lila's voice came again, but this time, it was softer, more fragile, as if she were trying to ease him into something she knew wouldn't work. "Jim… please. Let's not do this now. Dinner's ready, let's just eat—"

Her voice broke off with a sharp gasp. Ethan heard the unmistakable sound of something heavy hitting the floor, the thud of glass shattering against the tile. It was followed by a moment of silence—a terrifying moment where even the house seemed to hold its breath.

"Goddamn it, Lila!" Jim's roar shook the walls. Ethan could hear the fury in every syllable, the deep, hateful undercurrent that made his chest tighten. "This is your fault! I work my ass off for this family, and what do I get? A fucking mess!"

There was another crash—this time, louder. Ethan's body flinched as he heard the sound of a plate breaking, shards of porcelain scattering across the floor.

Lila's voice trembled as she pleaded, "Please, Jim… don't do this."

But it was too late. The storm had already hit.

Ethan's stomach churned. He had learned long ago that there was no reasoning with Jim when he was like this. His father's anger was a beast that couldn't be tamed, only weathered. And even though Lila tried—tried so hard to protect him—Ethan could see it. Her warmth, her love, it wasn't enough. Not when Jim's rage was like a wildfire, consuming everything in its path.

Lila's arms tightened around him as if she were trying to hold him together, her hands gently rubbing his back in the same comforting way she always had. Ethan could hear the desperation in her voice now, the way it cracked, the way she was trying to convince herself as much as him.

"Ethan," she whispered again, her voice shaking. "It's going to be okay. I'm here. I'll always protect you."

But Ethan knew better. He had seen the look in his mother's eyes too many times—the fear, the helplessness, the way she tried to hide her tears behind a smile. She couldn't protect them from Jim, not really. And no matter how tight she held him, he could feel the storm pressing in around them.

And just like that, it came—the sudden silence that followed the rage. It was worse than the yelling. It was the calm before the real damage. The tension in the air felt thick, suffocating.

Ethan's breath caught in his throat as Jim's footsteps thundered toward the living room, dragging his weight with every step. Ethan's heart raced as he tried to make himself as small as possible, curling into his mother's arms. He didn't want to see what came next. He didn't want to feel it.

But there it was—Jim's towering figure filling the doorway, his face flushed red, eyes wild with fury. The sight of him was enough to make Ethan's pulse spike. Jim's jaw clenched as he looked at them, and for a moment, Ethan could swear he saw a flicker of something in his father's eyes—something sharp, dangerous.

"You think you can keep hiding from me, Lila?" Jim's voice was a low growl, his words dripping with venom. "You can't protect him forever."

Ethan flinched, instinctively trying to shrink further into his mother's embrace, but Lila didn't let him go. Her hands were still warm, still holding him tight, but even she couldn't stop the fear that crept into her voice when she spoke again.

"Please, Jim," she whispered. "I'm just trying to keep us together. I'm trying to keep him safe."

Jim laughed bitterly, and the sound sent a shiver down Ethan's spine. "Safe? You think you're keeping him safe by coddling him? You're making him weak. And when he's weak, he'll end up just like me."

Ethan closed his eyes, not wanting to hear any more, but he couldn't stop it. The words cut through him like a blade, deep and unforgiving. His father's voice had always been a reminder of what he never wanted to become, of the man who had broken everything—his mother, his family, and, now, Ethan himself.

The anger hung in the air, suffocating everything around them, and Ethan could do nothing but sit there, helpless, in the shadow of it. All he wanted was to disappear. To escape it.

But even as he tried to imagine running away, he knew there was no place to run. Not when the storm followed them everywhere.

Ethan had been watching his mother's slow decline for what felt like an eternity. It wasn't sudden; it wasn't like one moment she was fine, and the next she was gone. It had been a gradual shift, a slow, creeping change in the way she moved, the way she smiled, the way she looked at him.

The first time Ethan noticed something wasn't right, she had been coughing a lot. Just a cold, the doctor said. But it didn't go away. A week stretched into two, then into a month. And then the bruises started to appear—dark patches on her arms, like someone had held her too tightly, like the illness was squeezing the life out of her, piece by piece.

Ethan had heard his father's angry voice late at night, his low growl of frustration as he tried to argue with his mother about seeing another doctor. Jim didn't believe in doctors, not the way his mother did. He refused to see how much she was suffering, how pale her skin had become, how weak her body seemed to be.

"It's just a phase," Jim would mutter when Ethan would ask about her. "She's just tired."

But Ethan knew better. He saw it in the way his mother's hands shook when she tried to make him breakfast, in the way she leaned against the doorframe when she called him in from outside to do his homework. Her warmth, once a constant in their small house, was fading. The light in her eyes was dimming.

And then, one cold autumn evening, after weeks of arguments and hushed conversations, his mother was admitted to the hospital.

The hospital room was sterile, too bright, and smelled of antiseptic. The harsh lights made Ethan squint as he stood in the doorway, his hand gripping the cold metal handle. His mother lay in the bed, her face a pale shadow of the woman she had once been. The sight made his heart ache, the love and tenderness he'd always known her to have, now hidden behind the machines and tubes that seemed to take up so much space around her.

Ethan had visited her every day after school, clutching his homework in one hand, his other hand pressed against the cool glass of the window as he looked at her, waiting for her to wake up, waiting for her to be the mother he remembered. But each day, she was weaker than before.

Her illness had been diagnosed as cancer—lung cancer, they said—but by the time they found it, it had already spread, like a shadow growing darker every day. It was a battle his mother couldn't fight, no matter how hard she tried to keep going for him. She was fading, slipping away in small, quiet moments.

The doctors had told them, softly and with sympathy in their voices, that there was little they could do. The treatments weren't working. There was no cure. But no one had told Ethan. They didn't need to. He could see it in his mother's eyes, in the way she no longer had the energy to argue with his father, the way she slept longer and longer, her breaths shallow and slow.

It was a Wednesday when the news came. Ethan sat by his mother's side, coloring in his notebook, like any other afternoon, pretending that everything was okay. His father had barely spoken to him, too wrapped up in his own anger and bitterness, but Ethan didn't mind. He'd gotten used to the silence between them. His mother's presence was all that mattered.

But then a nurse entered the room, her face tight with something Ethan couldn't name, and she told him that he needed to step outside for a moment. The air outside the hospital was colder than it had been in the past few weeks, biting at his skin, but it wasn't the cold that made his hands shake. It wasn't the wind, either. It was the look on the nurse's face. That look that told him more than any words could.

His legs felt heavy as he moved outside to the waiting area, his heart beating too fast, as though his body knew something he didn't want to acknowledge. It was in the hushed voices around him, in the way the staff walked by with their heads turned, not meeting his eyes. He couldn't bear it. He couldn't bear the waiting.

And then, just like that, it happened.

The hospital room seemed even quieter when Ethan returned. His mother, once the vibrant, loving woman who had been his whole world, was still. The machines that had been humming beside her now beeped erratically, the noise too sharp against the overwhelming silence. He stood frozen at the door, a cold chill crawling up his spine. Her hand, which he had held so many times before, was still.

"Mom?" His voice was small, fragile, and as soon as he spoke, he knew. He knew in the pit of his stomach that his mother wasn't going to wake up this time. She wouldn't smile at him, tell him everything would be okay, make him another peanut butter sandwich when he got home from school. The room was too empty, too still.

His father, Jim, finally showed up after what felt like hours. He walked in, his face hard as stone, but there was something in his eyes—something different. For the first time in what seemed like forever, Ethan saw something like... fear. Jim looked at his wife's body, then turned to Ethan, his voice low and strained. "She's gone, kid."

Ethan's world spun in that moment, the words hitting him like a punch. He couldn't breathe. He couldn't think. She couldn't be gone. Not his mom. Not like this.

For a long time, he didn't speak. His mouth was dry, his throat too tight. His body felt numb, as if it had forgotten how to move. He had no words for the storm swirling in his chest—there were no words that could explain the feeling of losing the one person who had ever really loved him.

But the silence didn't last. Jim was still there, looming over him like a shadow, his presence filling the empty space between them. His dad's voice was cold, detached. "Guess it's just you and me now, kid. No more of her. Just us."

The funeral was a blur. Ethan couldn't remember the faces of the people who showed up, didn't care who they were. His world had narrowed to the sound of the rain pattering against the windows of the house, to the smell of fresh-cut flowers that overwhelmed the room, to the hollow emptiness where his mother used to be.

She wasn't coming back. He wasn't sure he would ever be able to come to terms with it.

But the one thing that he knew for sure was that nothing would ever be the same again.

By the time Ethan turned thirteen, the house no longer felt like a home. It was just four walls holding together the weight of silence, anger, and regret. His father, Jim, had spiraled deeper into his drinking, the loss of Ethan's mother carving out a hole he tried to fill with cheap whiskey and bitter words. Ethan had long stopped trying to please him, the futile effort only met with frustration and, more often than not, the sharp sting of Jim's anger.

The nights were the worst. The sound of the front door slamming shut late in the evening was Ethan's signal to brace himself. He'd lie in bed, staring at the peeling paint on the ceiling, listening as Jim stumbled into the kitchen, muttering curses under his breath. Sometimes it was just noise—the clinking of bottles, the scrape of a chair on the floor. Other times, it was the loud, booming voice that made Ethan's stomach knot.

One night, Jim stormed into Ethan's room, the stench of alcohol thick in the air. "You think you're too good to help out around here?" he slurred, swaying slightly. Ethan had forgotten to take out the trash—again. The excuse died in his throat as Jim's voice rose, cutting through the quiet. "You're just like her. Weak."

The words stung more than the backhand that followed.

It was Grace who made things bearable.

She had been a constant in Ethan's life since they were kids, the girl who sat next to him in elementary school, who shared her crayons when his broke. But after his mother's death, Grace had become something more—a safe place, a friend who never asked too many questions but always seemed to know when he needed her most.

At school, Grace was the one who pulled him out of his shell, dragging him to sit with her and her friends at lunch, even when he'd much rather eat alone. She'd nudge him with her elbow, making silly jokes until he smiled.

"You know, if you keep frowning like that, your face is gonna stick that way," she teased one afternoon, leaning back against the cafeteria bench with a grin.

Ethan rolled his eyes, but there was a hint of a smile tugging at the corners of his mouth. "Better than smiling all the time. People might think I'm weird."

"Oh, Ethan," she sighed dramatically, her green eyes sparkling. "People already think you're weird. Might as well embrace it."

It was in these moments that Ethan felt normal, like the weight of his father's shadow wasn't looming over him. Grace had a way of making the world seem brighter, even when everything else felt like it was falling apart.

As the years went on, their friendship deepened. They'd spend hours at the lake just outside of town, sitting on the dock with their feet dangling in the water, talking about everything and nothing. Grace would tell him about her dreams of leaving the small town someday, of traveling to faraway places and doing something big with her life.

"What about you?" she asked one evening, her voice soft as the sun dipped below the horizon, painting the sky in hues of orange and pink. "What do you want, Ethan?"

He hesitated, staring out at the water. "I just... I just want to get out of here."

Grace looked at him, her expression unreadable. "And go where?"

"Anywhere. Somewhere I can breathe."

But as much as Ethan leaned on Grace, he kept the worst of his life hidden from her. She didn't know about the bruises, the nights he spent lying awake, trying to block out his father's yelling. He couldn't bring himself to tell her. Part of him was ashamed. The other part didn't want to see the pity in her eyes.

Still, Grace knew enough. She could see the exhaustion in his face, the way he flinched when someone raised their voice. And while she didn't press him for details, she made it her mission to be there for him.

One afternoon, when Ethan showed up at her house with a fresh cut on his lip, she didn't say a word. She simply handed him a glass of lemonade and pulled him out to the porch, where they sat in silence, watching the world go by.

"Whatever it is," she said after a long while, "you don't have to go through it alone."

Ethan didn't respond, but her words stayed with him, lingering in the back of his mind like a flicker of light in the darkness.

The more time Ethan spent with Grace, the harder it became to ignore the stark contrast between the life he had and the life he wanted. Grace represented hope, a future that didn't feel so heavy. But every time he returned home, that hope was crushed under the weight of his father's presence.

The abuse grew worse as Ethan got older, his father's anger fueled by jealousy and resentment. Jim saw Ethan not as a son, but as a reminder of his own failures—a boy who had the potential to escape the small town life that had trapped him.

The tipping point came on a cold winter night when Ethan was sixteen. Jim's rage had reached a boiling point, and for the first time, Ethan fought back. It wasn't much—a shove, a sharp word—but it was enough to send Jim over the edge.

That night, as the storm raged outside, Ethan made his decision. He couldn't stay. Not anymore.

The storm rolled in with a vengeance, clouds thick and black, churning in the sky as if mirroring the chaos brewing inside Ethan's home. Thunder growled low and distant at first, a warning, before it cracked loud enough to rattle the windows. Rain lashed against the roof in relentless sheets, the wind howling through the eaves like a feral thing.

Inside, Ethan stood frozen in the narrow hallway, his father's voice slurred and venomous as it filled the cramped space.

"You think you're better than me, don't you?" Jim spat, his words dripping with spite. The bottle in his hand swayed precariously as he pointed it at Ethan. "You've always thought that. Just like your mother. Always looking down on me."

"I'm not like you," Ethan said quietly, his fists clenched at his sides. His voice didn't waver, but his heart pounded in his chest like a drumbeat.

Jim's face twisted into a sneer, his lips curling as he took a step forward. "What'd you say to me, boy?"

Ethan didn't flinch, didn't move, even as his father closed the distance between them. He was done cowering. Done letting Jim's words tear him apart piece by piece. "I said I'm not like you."

For a moment, there was only silence, the storm outside providing a soundtrack to the charged stillness. And then Jim lashed out, his hand catching Ethan across the face with enough force to send him stumbling back against the wall.

But Ethan didn't cry out. He didn't run. He stood his ground, the sting on his cheek a small price to pay for the freedom he was about to claim.

"You're not worth a damn," Jim growled, the venom in his voice cutting deeper than the slap ever could. "You'll never make it out there. You're nothing."

Ethan's jaw tightened, his vision swimming with unshed tears. "You're wrong," he said, his voice barely above a whisper. "I don't need you. I never did."

Without waiting for a response, he turned on his heel and stormed up the stairs to his room. His hands shook as he threw open his closet, grabbing the backpack he'd stashed there months ago. It was already packed with the essentials—clothes, a little cash he'd saved from odd jobs, and a picture of his mother tucked safely into the front pocket.

Lightning lit up the sky as he zipped the bag shut and slung it over his shoulder. His hands hesitated for a moment on the strap, the weight of the decision pressing down on him. He took a deep breath, steeling himself.

There was nothing left for him here.

He crept down the stairs, avoiding the creaky spots he'd memorized over the years. Jim was passed out in the armchair, the bottle of whiskey dangling from his fingers. Ethan paused at the front door, his eyes flicking back to his father. For a brief moment, guilt wormed its way into his chest, but he pushed it aside.

The storm swallowed him whole as he stepped outside. The cold rain soaked him instantly, plastering his hair to his forehead and chilling him to the bone. But he didn't stop. His sneakers slapped against the wet pavement as he ran, his breaths coming in sharp gasps.

The storm hadn't eased, but Ethan didn't feel the cold rain soaking his clothes as he left the house. The door slammed shut behind him, muffled by the wind, and he knew he wouldn't be stepping back inside. Ever.

His feet carried him through the muddy streets, not toward the train station, but to the small house at the edge of town where Grace lived. Her house was easy to spot, even in the dark—its white paint glowing faintly under the streetlights, the curtains in her bedroom window drawn back just enough to let the golden light spill out.

He hesitated at the gate, his breath fogging in the chill air. He hadn't planned to say goodbye to anyone, least of all her. But the thought of leaving without seeing her one last time weighed too heavily.

Taking a deep breath, he walked up the short path and knocked softly on the door.

It opened moments later, revealing Grace in her flannel pajamas, her auburn hair loose around her shoulders. Her eyes widened when she saw him, concern flashing across her face.

"Ethan? What are you doing here?" she asked, her voice soft but urgent.

"I'm leaving," he said simply, the words tasting foreign on his tongue.

"What?" Grace stepped onto the porch, closing the door behind her. The storm whipped her hair around her face, but she didn't seem to notice. "What do you mean, leaving?"

He looked down, kicking at the wooden step with the toe of his shoe. "I can't stay here, Grace. Not with him. I've made up my mind."

Her hands tightened into fists at her sides, and for a moment, it looked like she might argue. But then her expression softened, her green eyes glistening with unshed tears. "Where will you go?"

"Anywhere but here," he said with a faint, humorless smile. "I'll figure it out."

Grace stepped closer, her voice trembling. "Ethan, you don't have to do this alone. You could stay here. With me. My parents would understand—they'd help you."

He shook his head, his throat tightening. "It's not your problem, Grace. You've already done so much for me. But this… this is something I have to do for myself."

She stared at him for a long moment, the storm raging around them, before throwing her arms around his neck. Her warmth, her scent—everything about her—made him want to stay. Made him want to believe things could be different.

"I'll miss you," she whispered, her voice breaking.

Ethan closed his eyes, holding her tightly. "I'll miss you, too."

When she pulled back, there was a determination in her gaze that made his heart ache. "Promise me something."

"Anything," he said without hesitation.

"Promise me you won't forget this place. Or me."

He swallowed hard, the lump in his throat nearly choking him. "I promise."

For a moment, it seemed like she might kiss him. Her eyes lingered on his, her lips parting slightly. But instead, she stepped back, her arms falling to her sides.

"Goodbye, Ethan," she said, her voice barely audible over the storm.

"Goodbye, Grace."

The station was nearly empty when he arrived, the fluorescent lights casting a harsh glow on the cracked tile floors. A single clerk sat behind the ticket counter, looking bored as she flipped through a magazine. Ethan approached, his heart still racing.

"One ticket, please," he said, his voice hoarse.

The clerk glanced up, her brows raising as she took in his disheveled appearance. "Where to?"

"Doesn't matter," Ethan replied. "Just the next train out."

She frowned but didn't argue, printing the ticket and sliding it across the counter. "Platform two. Leaves in ten minutes."

Ethan nodded, clutching the ticket tightly as he made his way to the platform. The rain had slowed to a drizzle, the storm beginning to move on, but the air was still electric, heavy with the promise of change.

As the train pulled into the station, its wheels screeching against the tracks, Ethan felt a strange mix of fear and exhilaration. He was leaving behind everything he'd ever known—his father, his mother's memory, Grace.

Grace.

Her name echoed in his mind as he stepped onto the train, finding an empty seat by the window. He stared out at the rain-slicked platform, his chest tightening. For a moment, he wondered what she'd think when she realized he was gone.

But he couldn't stay. Not even for her.

The train lurched forward, the station falling away into the night. Ethan leaned his head against the window, watching the dark countryside blur past. He didn't know what the future held, but for the first time in his life, he felt something that had always seemed just out of reach.

Freedom.

Chapter Three

Ethan's first real glimpse of Gulf City came in the early hours of dawn, when the rain had finally stopped and the sun began creeping up over the skyline. The towering buildings were a patchwork of cracked windows and shining glass, a blend of the old and new. Street vendors were already setting up, their carts sending up smells of sizzling meat and spices. The city was alive in a way Ashville never was, but it also felt indifferent, like it wouldn't notice if he vanished into its shadows.

His first night was spent on a park bench, his duffel bag doubling as a pillow. He tried to sleep, but the cold and the sounds of the city—sirens, distant shouting, the steady hum of traffic—kept him awake. Hunger clawed at his stomach, but there was nothing he could do.

By his second day, Ethan wandered the streets looking for work. The desperation in his voice must have been obvious when he asked shopkeepers if they needed help. Some ignored him, others waved him away, and one barked at him to "get lost, kid."

Ethan had been in the city a week when he met Joe. The food truck owner was a fixture near the park, his truck a beacon of warmth on chilly nights. Ethan approached hesitantly, eyeing the sign advertising hot dogs and fries. He didn't have enough money for even the cheapest item.

Joe noticed him lingering. "You gonna order, or just stare all night?"

"Sorry," Ethan muttered, turning to leave.

"Hold on," Joe called out. "You look like you could use a bite. On the house."

The hot dog was the best thing Ethan had eaten in weeks. He devoured it in minutes, barely pausing to breathe.

"You're new around here," Joe said, handing him a bottle of water. "You got family?"

"No."

Joe didn't ask any more questions, but from that night on, Ethan became a regular at the food truck. Joe never asked for payment, though Ethan started doing small tasks for him—hauling crates, cleaning up after the lunch rush.

"Kid, you're tougher than you look," Joe said once, slapping him on the back. "Stick around. This city might just grow on you."

It was a cold November night when Ethan crossed paths with Marcus, a man whose gold tooth caught the light every time he grinned. Ethan had been walking through a quiet stretch of downtown, looking for his next odd job, when Marcus stepped out of an alley.

"You looking for work?" Marcus asked, his tone friendly but his eyes sharp.

Ethan hesitated. "Depends on the job."

Marcus leaned in, his grin widening. "Simple stuff. Moving things, no questions asked. Pays good."

The offer was tempting—Ethan hadn't eaten in two days—but something about Marcus set him on edge. "I'm good, thanks," he said, starting to walk away.

Marcus's hand shot out, grabbing his arm. "Think carefully, kid. Not everyone gets a second chance."

Ethan wrenched his arm free and ran, his heart pounding as he turned corner after corner. He didn't stop until he was back in the safety of Joe's food truck.

"You look like you've seen a ghost," Joe said, handing him a cup of coffee.

"Something like that," Ethan muttered.

Ethan was sixteen when Maria found him sleeping in the laundry room of a run-down motel. He had been working odd jobs for weeks, but the money was never enough for a proper place to stay. The laundry room had been warm and quiet, and Ethan had thought he could get a few hours of rest before anyone noticed.

Maria walked in with a basket of sheets and stopped short when she saw him. For a moment, Ethan expected her to yell, to call the manager and have him thrown out. Instead, she set the basket down and said, "You look like you need a meal."

"I'll leave," Ethan said quickly, grabbing his bag.

"Stay," she said gently. "You hungry?"

Maria didn't just give him food; she gave him advice. "This city will chew you up if you let it," she told him, sliding a plate of rice and beans across the table. "But if you keep your head up, you'll find people who care."

Ethan started helping her with small tasks around the motel, fixing broken fixtures and carrying linens. She paid him what she could and always made sure he had something to eat.

"You've got a good soul, niño," she told him one day. "Don't let anyone take that from you."

It was Clara who gave Ethan his first real chance. She was in her sixties, her workshop filled with furniture in various states of repair. Ethan had been passing by when he saw her struggling to carry a heavy table.

"Need a hand?" he asked.

Clara squinted at him, her gray hair pulled back in a bun. "You any good with tools?"

"I can learn," Ethan said.

She paid him in cash that first day and asked him to come back the next morning. Over time, she taught him how to sand wood, fix broken legs, and polish old furniture until it looked brand new.

"You've got a knack for this," Clara said one afternoon, watching as Ethan worked on a chair. "Ever think about sticking around?"

Ethan smiled, the first genuine smile in weeks. "Maybe."

With Clara's help, Ethan began to rebuild his life. He found steadier work and rented a small room above a bakery. Nights were still lonely, but the memory of Grace kept him grounded. He wrote letters to her he never sent, pouring out his thoughts on crumpled pieces of paper that he tucked away in a shoebox.

Gulf City had changed him. The boy who had arrived with nothing was gone, replaced by someone stronger, more determined. But deep down, he knew he wasn't whole. Part of him was still in Ashville, still sitting on that train platform, saying goodbye to the only person who had ever truly understood him.

Ethan sat on the windowsill of his tiny room, the scent of freshly baked bread wafting up from the bakery below. It was late—too late to be awake, but the city seemed to hum differently at night, a quieter energy that helped him think.

In his lap was a notebook, its pages filled with letters he had no intention of sending. He tapped his pen against the page, staring at the half-written words.

Grace, he had started.
It's been two years since I left Ashville. I wonder if you ever think about that night. I wonder if you hate me for leaving. I wonder if you even remember me at all.

He sighed and closed the notebook, sliding it back into the shoebox where it joined dozens of others. No matter how much progress he made in Gulf City, there was a part of him that always drifted back to Ashville. To Grace.

Clara had become more than just an employer; she was a mentor, a steady presence in Ethan's chaotic life. One afternoon, as they worked side by side in her workshop, she looked up from the table she was sanding and said, "You've got a lot on your mind today."

Ethan hesitated, then shrugged. "Just thinking about where I came from. Feels like a lifetime ago."

Clara nodded, her hands never pausing in their rhythmic motion. "You ever talk to anyone about it?"

"Not really," Ethan admitted. "Doesn't seem like it'd change anything."

"Maybe not," Clara said, "but carrying it around forever doesn't help, either. Sometimes you have to let yourself feel it, or it'll eat you alive."

Ethan didn't respond, but her words stuck with him. That night, he found himself walking through the city aimlessly, the weight of his past heavier than ever.

It was a chance encounter that changed everything. A local gallery owner had stopped by Clara's shop, looking for unique pieces for an upcoming show. Ethan had been working on a small coffee table, its surface intricately carved with patterns he had improvised.

"This is beautiful," the gallery owner said, running her fingers over the polished wood.

"Thanks," Ethan said, startled by the compliment.

"You made this?"

He nodded.

The gallery owner offered to display the piece in her show, and though Ethan was reluctant, Clara encouraged him to say yes. "You've got talent, kid," she said. "It's time people saw it."

The coffee table sold within hours of the gallery opening. The buyer left a business card and an offer for more commissions. For the first time, Ethan felt like he was truly building something.

Despite his growing success, Ethan couldn't shake the memory of Grace. He found himself returning to places in Gulf City that reminded him of her—a small bookstore that smelled like the one they used to visit after school, a park bench where the light hit just right, like the tree they used to sit under.

One day, while walking through the city, he saw a young couple laughing together on a street corner. The girl's laugh was high and musical, just like Grace's. It stopped him in his tracks, a pang of longing twisting in his chest.

He leaned against a nearby wall, trying to steady his breathing. He had left Ashville to escape the pain, but sometimes it felt like he had brought it with him, tucked away in the corners of his mind.

Years passed, and Ethan became a man who no longer resembled the scared boy who had run away from home. He had his own business now, crafting furniture that was sought after by collectors and designers. He had friends, a modest apartment, and a life he could be proud of.

But there were nights when the city felt too big, too loud, and he would sit by the window, staring at the skyline and thinking about the little town he had left behind.

One evening, as he closed up his workshop, he found a letter waiting for him in his mailbox. It was from Joe, the food truck owner who had given him his first meal in Gulf City. Inside was a short note:

Ethan,
I've been following your work. You've come a long way, kid. But don't forget—sometimes the things we leave behind are the ones that matter most.

The words hit him harder than he expected. He folded the letter carefully and placed it in his pocket. That night, he didn't sleep.

Ethan worked late into the night, his hands calloused and steady as he shaped wood into something elegant and lasting. His workshop smelled of sawdust and varnish, a small sanctuary carved out of the chaos of the city. The space was a testament to the long road he had traveled to get here—years of scraping by, of being nameless, of surviving.

Sometimes, when the world went quiet, he let himself remember Ashville. Not the dark memories of his father or the echo of his mother's absence, but the lighter ones: Grace laughing as she tossed a skipping stone into the lake, her voice cutting through the stillness like sunlight through clouds. Those moments were rare now, fleeting like shadows at dusk.

One evening, Clara stopped by the shop. The old woman had been a lifeline during Ethan's hardest days, offering odd jobs and, eventually, a corner of her garage to store his tools.

"You're burning the midnight oil again," she said, carrying a thermos of coffee and a plate of biscuits. "Thought you could use a break."

Ethan smirked, setting down the plane he had been using. "I could always use a break. Thanks, Clara."

She lingered, her sharp eyes scanning the room before settling on him. "You've come a long way, Ethan. But every time I see you working like this, I wonder what it is you're chasing."

"I'm not chasing anything," he replied, though the words felt hollow.

Clara tilted her head. "Maybe not. But something's chasing you."

Ethan didn't respond, letting the silence stretch between them. After a moment, Clara gave his shoulder a squeeze and left him to his thoughts.

That night, Ethan found himself pulling out the shoebox from the bottom drawer of his desk. It was scuffed and dented, packed with unsent letters, each one addressed to Grace. Some were only a few lines long; others sprawled across pages.

He picked up a fresh piece of paper and began writing, his hand moving without hesitation.

Grace,
I don't know where to start. I guess I never do. I've written this letter a hundred times, and I never seem to get it right. But tonight, it feels different. Maybe because I keep thinking about the way you smiled when we were kids. How everything felt simpler back then, even when it wasn't.

I left because I had to, but it doesn't mean I don't think about what I left behind. You were the one good thing in all of it, and I never told you that. I should have. I should have told you a lot of things.

He paused, the pen hovering over the paper, then set it down. The weight of the words was too much to bear. Carefully, he folded the letter and slipped it into the box, where it joined the others. He snapped the lid shut and shoved it back into the drawer.

The letters would never see the light of day. Grace belonged to a life he had left behind, one he could never return to.

And yet, as he lay in bed that night, her face lingered in his mind, more vivid than it had been in years.

The city had a way of swallowing people whole. Its streets buzzed with life at every hour, the kind of constant motion that made the days blur together and the years pass unnoticed. For Ethan, Gulf City had become a rhythm, a routine he no longer questioned.

At first, the memories of Ashville had clung to him like the scent of pine after a storm—sharp and inescapable. He could still see Grace's face if he closed his eyes, hear her laugh echoing in his mind. But over time, the edges of those memories softened, like the fraying threads of an old quilt. He no longer flinched at the thought of his father or winced at the image of his mother's hollow eyes. Instead, those memories became like faded photographs: important, but distant.

Ethan's work became his anchor. His small business had grown from a one-man operation to a thriving workshop with a steady stream of clients. Custom furniture orders poured in, each one more intricate than the last. His hands were never idle, and for the first time in years, his mind wasn't either.

The people he had once considered passing acquaintances now felt like family. Clara, who still stopped by with coffee and unsolicited advice. Manuel, a gruff yet kind-hearted contractor who had been one of Ethan's first big clients. Even Bree, the owner of a nearby café, who always had a knack for knowing when he needed a quiet place to sit and think.

One Friday evening, Bree leaned against the counter as Ethan sipped a cup of black coffee at the bar. The café was quiet, the hum of conversations reduced to a gentle murmur in the background.

"You're finally starting to look comfortable," she teased, sliding him a second biscuit.

Ethan chuckled. "Comfortable? That's a first."

"No, I mean it," she said, studying him with a thoughtful expression. "When you first showed up, you looked like a man who was just... passing through. Like you had one foot out the door."

Ethan paused, stirring his coffee. "And now?"

"Now?" Bree smiled. "Now you look like you've put down roots. This place suits you."

He didn't respond right away, letting her words sink in. She was right, in a way. The city no longer felt foreign. The noise, the hustle—it was home now.

But late at night, when the world quieted, Ethan would sometimes reach for the shoebox in his drawer. He rarely opened it anymore, and even when he did, the letters felt like they belonged to someone else. A boy who had once believed in second chances, in the idea that some part of his old life could be salvaged.

Now, those thoughts felt naive. Grace had probably moved on, just as he had. Ashville was a distant memory, a chapter he had closed long ago.

The next morning, Ethan stood in his workshop, running his fingers over the grain of a nearly finished table. The piece was destined for a wealthy client's dining room, a centerpiece for family gatherings and celebrations. It was his finest work yet, and it reminded him how far he had come.

"Good work," Manuel said, clapping him on the back. "You've built something real here, Ethan."

Ethan nodded, his gaze steady. "Yeah. I guess I have."

For the first time in years, the weight of his past felt lighter. Gulf City was his home now. The people here were his family. And though the threads of Ashville and Grace still lingered in the back of his mind, they no longer defined him.

He was Ethan Blackwell, a man who had carved out a life of his own. And for now, that was enough.

Ethan stood outside Clara's old furniture repair shop, now bearing a sleek sign with the name "Haven Restorations" in bold, modern lettering. The shop was unrecognizable from the dusty, cluttered place it had been when Clara first took him in. Back then, her generosity had been the only thing keeping the doors open—along with her stubborn refusal to give up on her little piece of the city.

Now, Ethan had turned it into a thriving business. The small space had expanded into the adjoining storefront, and the workshop buzzed with the sound of sanding, sawing, and crafting. It was a far cry from the days when Clara would sit behind the counter, nursing a cup of coffee and worrying about bills.

"I never thought I'd see this place like this," Clara said, standing beside him. Her eyes had a wistful gleam, a mix of pride and nostalgia. "You've done more than I ever dreamed."

Ethan smiled, but his voice softened. "I wouldn't have had a chance if you hadn't taken me in."

Clara shook her head. "You earned your way, Ethan. Don't let anyone tell you different."

Inside, Maria bustled near the counter, organizing invoices and answering calls. She'd started working for Ethan a few years ago when he expanded, and her knack for keeping things in order had been invaluable.

"I've got the delivery schedule sorted," Maria called, her voice cutting through the workshop's hum. "You're set for next week, boss."

Ethan chuckled. "How many times do I have to tell you not to call me that?"

Maria grinned. "You can't stop me. You're the boss, so you'll just have to live with it."

Later that afternoon, Ethan made his way to Joe's food truck, parked in its usual spot near the corner of Sixth and Main. The smell of grilled meat and spices filled the air as customers lined up for lunch. Joe waved him over with a spatula in hand.

"Ethan! Haven't seen you in a while," Joe called, his face breaking into a grin.

"Been busy at the shop," Ethan replied, stepping to the side of the truck. He handed Joe a check.

Joe glanced at it, his brow furrowing. "What's this for?"

Ethan shrugged. "For everything you did back then. You gave me food when I couldn't afford it. Let me pay you back."

Joe shook his head, pushing the check back toward Ethan. "You already did that, kid. Look at you now. That's enough for me."

Ethan sighed, pocketing the check but making a mental note to find another way to pay it forward. Joe had always been stubborn, but Ethan wasn't giving up.

Ethan leaned back in his office chair, gazing at the row of neatly restored chairs lining the workshop wall. Each one told a story—a family heirloom saved from decay, a discarded relic brought back to life. This shop, this city, had become his story. Yet, some days, he felt the faint pull of something unresolved, like a book left open to its middle pages.

He closed the ledger in front of him and glanced at the clock. It was nearly 6 p.m., time to lock up and grab dinner. Maria waved as she headed out, her ever-efficient demeanor softened by a rare smile.

"Don't work too late," she called, slipping her bag over her shoulder.

"I won't," Ethan lied, already eyeing the unfinished table in the corner.

Once the shop was empty, Ethan found himself staring out the large front window. The city buzzed with its usual life—horns honking, people chatting, the hum of progress. He loved it here, but tonight, he couldn't shake the memory of another window from years ago, cracked and grimy, with storm clouds rolling in behind it.

The past had a funny way of creeping in when you least expected it. Grace's laugh echoed faintly in his mind, followed by the sharp bark of his father's anger. Two opposing forces, each pulling him in different directions.

Shaking his head, he grabbed his jacket and headed out. Joe's food truck was still open, the faint glow of string lights giving it an inviting warmth.

"Back again?" Joe teased as Ethan approached.

"Don't act so surprised," Ethan replied, handing over a few bills.

Joe handed him a sandwich and leaned on the counter. "You ever think about writing a book? You've got the look of someone with stories to tell."

Ethan gave a half-smile. "Maybe one day. But not yet."

Joe nodded knowingly. "Not ready to dig up the old stuff?"

Ethan didn't respond. Instead, he bit into his sandwich, letting the savory flavors distract him. But as he walked home through the bustling streets, he couldn't shake the feeling that the past was circling closer.

The next morning, Ethan was in the middle of sanding a custom table when his phone buzzed. He glanced at the screen, unfamiliar with the number, but something in his gut told him to answer.

"Hello?"

"Mr. Blackwell? This is Carolyn Dempsey from Ashville Law Associates. I'm calling regarding your late father's estate. We need you to come back to finalize some legal matters."

Ethan froze, the sander still running in his hand. The noise droned on, but his mind raced. Ashville. The name alone was enough to send a cold chill down his spine.

"I don't think you understand," Ethan said, his voice tight. "There's nothing there for me."

"I understand, Mr. Blackwell," Carolyn replied, her tone professional but firm. "However, as the sole legal heir, it's your responsibility to handle the estate. We've been trying to reach you for weeks. This cannot wait any longer."

Ethan shut off the sander and stared at the half-finished table, his jaw clenched.

"How long do I have?" he asked finally.

"A week at most," Carolyn said. "I'll email you the details."

When the call ended, Ethan sat in silence, the weight of the conversation sinking in. He thought he'd left Ashville behind for good. Now it seemed the town wasn't done with him.

Ethan stood in his office, staring out the window as the sun dipped below the horizon. He had never imagined this day would come. Ashville. The very thought of it made his stomach tighten, and yet, here he was, preparing for a trip that would take him back to the place he'd vowed to leave behind forever.

The phone call had been clear: he had no choice. The estate needed settling, the paperwork finalized. As the only living relative, he was the one to handle it. And so, after years of building a life that was as far from Ashville as possible, he was going back.

He turned away from the window, snapping his mind back to the task at hand. He moved across the room, gathering his things from the desk—his phone, his wallet, a few important documents that might come in handy. He needed to get the details right. The business could continue without him, but he had to make sure it ran smoothly while he was gone.

He picked up the phone and dialed Maria's number first. She picked up after the second ring.

"Maria, hey. I'm going to need you to take over scheduling while I'm gone. Make sure everything's running on track with the new contracts. You know what to do."

"Got it, Mr. Blackwell," she replied. There was a brief pause before she added, "Be careful. Don't hesitate to call if you need anything."

"Thanks. I'll be fine," Ethan said, though he knew better. He couldn't shake the tightness in his chest, the gnawing feeling that this trip would dredge up more than just business.

He hung up and moved to the next task. Clara.

He dialed her number next.

"Clara, I need you to hold down the fort while I'm away. You'll be in charge while I'm gone. Any issues, you handle it. I trust you."

"I've got it, Ethan," Clara said. "Take care of whatever you need to do. We'll keep things running here."

He exhaled, already feeling the weight lifting off his shoulders. Clara had been with him from the beginning, and he knew she could keep things in line.

With those details squared away, it was time to pack. He didn't need much—just enough to get him through a few days. As he pulled his suitcase out of the closet, his hand brushed over the edge of the worn shoebox under his desk. His heart skipped a beat, his fingers hesitating before brushing it aside.

It was there—the box of unsent letters. His heart tugged at the thought of them, but he quickly turned his attention elsewhere. Packing.

Shirts. Jeans. A jacket. He folded his clothes methodically, his mind racing as the minutes passed.

And then, there it was. The familiar rustling of paper. His hand reached instinctively for the box. As he pulled it from under the desk, the lid popped open, spilling letters across the floor. The edges of the pages were dog-eared from years of being shoved away—letters never sent, words never spoken.

He stood still, staring at them, as the memories came flooding back.

Some of the letters were old. Letters written years ago, full of raw emotion and unanswered questions. A few had Grace's name on them, though he never had the courage to send them. Each letter was a moment in time, frozen in his past.

Ethan sank down to the floor, slowly picking through the letters. His fingers hovered over one—its words as familiar as the sound of Grace's laugh. He could feel the weight of all those unspoken things, all those years he'd spent wondering.

What if?

Could he still go back? Would it even matter?

The thought lingered in his mind, and for a moment, it felt like he could hear Grace's voice calling him. But the harsh reality of his life in Gulf City tugged him back.

He quickly shoved the letters back into the box and closed the lid with a snap.

His gaze lingered for a moment longer, the past threatening to pull him in. But he forced himself to focus. There were more important things to do.

Ethan stood, wiped his hands against his pants, and took a deep breath. He had a flight to catch. There was no time for hesitation.

But the shoebox—the letters—remained on the floor, a reminder of a past he couldn't seem to shake.

He had no idea what he was walking into when he returned to Ashville. But the thought of Grace—and those letters—kept nagging at him, like a distant whisper in the back of his mind.

Chapter Four

Ethan stood at the doorway of his apartment, suitcase in hand. The weight of the bag was nothing compared to the weight in his chest, the quiet ache that had followed him for years. His eyes drifted back to the shoebox on the floor. He hadn't realized how long he'd been standing there, staring at it. It felt like an eternity, as if his past was calling to him, pulling him back in a way that he couldn't ignore.

He exhaled slowly, trying to shake the feeling, but the truth was, it had never really gone away. Grace. His mother. Ashville. The memories flooded back, overwhelming him with emotions he thought he had buried long ago.

He glanced at the shoebox, now tucked away again under his desk, but his thoughts lingered on it. On her. The letters he never sent. The words he never said. The path he chose, and the one he never took.

But the past was behind him, right? He'd made his choice. He'd walked away from it all. This was business. He had to focus on that, not the ghosts of his past.

Still, he felt the familiar pull of regret, even though he didn't want to admit it. He could almost hear Grace's voice in the back of his mind, telling him not to go, not to leave everything behind.

With a quiet sigh, Ethan turned away from the shoebox and picked up his keys. His apartment felt empty, too quiet—no distractions, no noise, nothing. Just him and the memories.

He walked to the door, taking one last glance at the space he had made his own. Gulf City had become his home in every sense of the word. But Ashville… Ashville had never truly left him.

Shaking off the thoughts, he closed the door behind him, the final click of the lock echoing in the silence.

As he drove to the airport, the city he had worked so hard to make his home felt distant. Gulf City was where he belonged now, wasn't it? The work, the people, the life he had built for himself—it was all here. Yet, as the car turned onto the highway, a part of him couldn't help but wonder what awaited him back in Ashville.

He would be there for a few days, just enough time to take care of the estate. The lawyer had made it clear: he needed to finalize everything. Once it was over, he would return to his life here, in the city where he had made his name.

But as he pulled up to the airport, the memories of Ashville lingered. His father's house. The streets. The faces of people he had once known. Grace.

He wasn't going to return to her. He wasn't going to look for her. But somehow, deep down, he couldn't shake the thought that maybe—just maybe—this trip wouldn't be as simple as he had hoped.

He stepped out of the car, his eyes lingering on the gates of the airport as he forced his thoughts forward. He had a flight to catch. The past would have to wait.

The small town of Ashville hadn't changed much over the years. The same faded storefronts lined the main street, the same quiet, sleepy atmosphere hung in the air. As Ethan drove through, it all felt strangely familiar and foreign at once. The town that had once felt like a cage now seemed like a distant memory—a place he had escaped, buried under years of success and new identities. But the truth lingered in the back of his mind, like an old scar that never quite healed.

He arrived at the law office, the familiar hum of the small town filling the air as he stepped inside. The walls were decorated with old family photos, legal certificates, and dusty bookshelves lined with decades of paperwork. The scent of paper and aging wood filled his nostrils as he was led into a small conference room.

The lawyer, a thin man with glasses perched on the edge of his nose, stood and extended his hand. "Mr. Blackwell. It's good to see you again. We'll make this quick."

Ethan nodded, his face blank. There was no need for pleasantries. He had been told over the phone exactly what would be required. He took a seat and let the lawyer do the talking. The paperwork was simple—just signatures and brief statements confirming the terms of the estate. The house, the land, and the assets had all been left in his name. It was his now, though it felt like a hollow victory.

As the lawyer explained everything, Ethan's mind wandered. The words came and went, but his thoughts were a tangled mess of memories. Clara's voice echoed in his head, the soft, steady way she had told him all those years ago to stop running. "You can't run forever, Ethan," she had said. "There's always a time when you have to face what you're running from."

And then there was Joe's voice, gruff but full of wisdom. "It's not about escaping, kid. It's about making peace with what happened."

Both voices seemed to call out from the past, as though the people who had helped him rebuild his life in Gulf City were there with him now. Would they have told him to come back here? To face the place he had run from so many years ago?

The weight of the question pressed on his chest. He could feel it deep inside him, an unease he couldn't shake. Would seeing the house again give him the closure he had long denied? Or would it only open old wounds that had never truly healed?

The lawyer finished explaining the final details of the paperwork, and Ethan stood up. "That's all?" he asked, his voice distant.

The lawyer nodded. "Yes. All that's left is for you to decide what you want to do with the property. We'll send the documents to your address in Gulf City."

Ethan barely heard him. He nodded absentmindedly and made his way out of the office. His steps felt heavier now, weighed down by the ghosts of the past, the echoes of his own regrets.

As he stepped outside into the crisp afternoon air, he paused for a moment. His gaze shifted down the street toward the house. The old Blackwell home—now his home. It sat on the edge of the town, looking much the same as it had when he was a child, though it felt somehow distant now. A house full of pain and memories, a place where his mother had once tried so hard to protect him from the chaos his father had created.

Ethan had avoided this place for years. He had driven past it countless times, but never stopped. The house was a reminder of everything he had escaped from—the nights of fear, the silent screams that echoed through the walls, the desperate feeling of being trapped. It was the source of his nightmares and the reason he had fled all those years ago.

But now, as he stood on the edge of the street, staring at the house, something shifted. A flicker of something deep inside him stirred. Maybe it was time to face it. To confront the past, and maybe, just maybe, put it to rest once and for all.

Without a word, he turned and walked toward the house, each step bringing him closer to a past he had tried so hard to forget. The front door stood open, as if waiting for him.

He stepped inside, and the house felt like it hadn't changed a bit. The smell of old wood, dust, and something faintly metallic filled the air. The silence was deafening, broken only by the sound of his own footsteps on the hardwood floor.

Ethan moved through the rooms, each one reminding him of something—of his mother's gentle touch, his father's fury, the way he had learned to hide in the corners and avoid the fights. He paused at the foot of the stairs, looking up at the empty hallways that had once been filled with tension and fear.

This place was both foreign and familiar, like a place in a dream he had long forgotten but was now forced to remember. His fingers brushed against the railing as he ascended the stairs, moving toward his old room. The door creaked open with a sound that felt like a distant echo from another life.

He stood there, in the doorway of the room where it had all started, where the boy he used to be had lived and dreamed of escape. The walls were still the same, though faded with time, but the bed was gone, and the posters on the walls had been replaced by dust. It was as if the house itself had been frozen in time, waiting for him to come back and take what was his.

Ethan took a long breath, his chest tightening. He didn't know what he was hoping for—closure, peace, maybe just a moment to confront the place that had shaped him into the person he was today.

But there was no answer here. There was no magic moment where everything made sense. Just silence.

As he stepped back into the hall and closed the door behind him, he felt something shift within him. He wasn't sure what it was, but the weight that had hung over him for so long felt a little lighter. Maybe it wasn't about running anymore. Maybe it was about moving forward.

Ethan stood there, his chest tight as the weight of the moment settled around him. The house that had once been his prison now felt like a strange, foreign place—made all the more surreal by Grace's unexpected presence. He had come here hoping to confront the past, to put it behind him. Instead, he was facing her, the one person who had always been tied to it, the one person he had left without a word. The one person who had always known him better than he knew himself.

His breath hitched as he looked at her, taking in the subtle changes in her appearance. She was still Grace—her hair a little longer now, her eyes a little softer—but there was something more in the way she carried herself. A quiet strength, perhaps, or a sense of calm that he hadn't seen in her all those years ago.

She had always been the one to ground him, even when he was running. And now, just as unexpectedly as when he'd left, she was here. The way she always seemed to show up when he needed her most.

"I didn't think anyone would be here," Ethan said again, his voice quieter this time. It was hard to make sense of what was happening. Was this just coincidence? Was it fate, as she'd said? Or something else entirely?

Grace's gaze softened, her smile carrying a hint of sadness. "Not many people are left. But I guess I never really left, either." She glanced around the room, her fingers still tucked into her jacket pockets. "Not in the way that matters."

Ethan didn't know what to say. His mind was a whirlwind of thoughts, memories, and emotions that he had spent so long burying. He had left this place, this town, and everything connected to it, thinking that distance would make the pain disappear. But now, standing here, with Grace in front of him, everything came rushing back.

"Why are you here?" Ethan asked, though he already knew the answer.

Grace hesitated, her eyes flickering to the old furniture, the same dusty walls that had once trapped them both. "I guess… I just wanted to be here for you. In case you needed someone. I know this place—it's hard to come back to."

His throat tightened as the weight of her words hit him. She wasn't asking for anything, wasn't expecting anything from him. She was simply offering her presence, a gesture of kindness that he had always taken for granted. She had been there when things had fallen apart, and now, here she was again, showing up when he had no idea what to do next.

He swallowed the lump in his throat, trying to push past the confusion swirling in his chest. "I didn't come here for that," he said, the words coming out more harshly than he intended. He cleared his throat, trying again. "I came to take care of things. The estate. The house. It's all just paperwork."

Grace nodded, her eyes not leaving his. "I know," she said, her voice soft. "But it's never just about paperwork, is it?"

Ethan looked at her, unsure of how to respond. How could he explain the years of running, the years of trying to build a life far away from this town, far away from all the pain? The truth was, he had been avoiding this moment for so long, pushing it down, pretending it didn't matter. But now, with Grace standing in front of him, everything seemed to matter all at once.

Her presence felt like a thread pulling him back to the person he had been before he left Ashville—the person who had cared, who had hoped, who had dreamed of a different life. But now, that person seemed like a stranger.

The silence between them stretched on, heavy and filled with unspoken things. Grace glanced around the room again, as if searching for something—answers, perhaps, or just the right words to say. Ethan's chest tightened as he realized how much had changed between them.

"I didn't think I'd ever come back here," he said quietly, almost to himself. "I didn't think I'd ever face this again."

Grace stepped closer, her gaze steady. "Sometimes we don't get to choose when or how we face things. Sometimes, it's just about showing up."

Her words landed like a truth he wasn't ready to hear. But there they were—simple, quiet, but undeniable. Grace had shown up, as she always had, even when he had left without a word. Even when he had thought he was better off without her.

"I don't know what I'm supposed to do now," he admitted, his voice rough. "I thought I could just... close the door on all this. On this town, on the past."

Grace didn't answer right away. She simply looked at him, her eyes filled with understanding. And then, in the quiet of that old house, she said something that caught him off guard.

"You don't have to close the door, Ethan," she said softly. "Maybe you just need to walk through it. Let yourself feel whatever you need to feel."

Ethan felt something shift inside him at her words. He hadn't realized how much he had been running, how much he had buried until right then, standing there with her. He had thought that leaving Ashville, leaving the house, would be enough. But it wasn't. And maybe it never would be.

For a long moment, neither of them spoke. It was as if the house had quieted, holding its breath, waiting for something. Ethan wasn't sure what that something was. He wasn't sure if he was ready for it, or if he ever would be.

But there Grace stood, as if time had never passed, as if nothing had changed. She was still the person who had cared, who had been there for him when no one else had. And in that moment, standing in the house that had once held so much pain, that was enough.

As they stood in the silence, the past, present, and future seemed to converge, and Ethan finally realized that maybe he hadn't been ready to leave Ashville after all. Maybe he had come back for a reason.

And as his gaze met Grace's, a quiet, unspoken understanding passed between them—neither of them knew what the future held, but for the first time in years, Ethan wasn't sure he needed to run anymore.

The air in the house was heavy with the scent of dust and forgotten years. The walls, once filled with the sounds of laughter and warmth, now seemed to echo only the silence left behind. Ethan stood in the doorway, a reluctant guest in the space that had shaped so much of who he had become—the place he had spent the worst and best years of his life. It was strange, how something so familiar could feel so foreign after all this time.

He hadn't planned on coming back to this house. Not now. Not like this. The paperwork was done—his mother's estate, his father's debts, everything settled, the house now his once again. But as he stood there, his hand resting on the doorframe, the weight of what was left to do hung over him like a storm cloud.

His gaze swept over the living room—the same furniture that had been there for years, the same cracks in the walls, the faint marks on the floor where things had been moved and rearranged. The place hadn't changed much. It hadn't had the chance to.

Ethan stepped into the room, his shoes scraping against the wooden floor. The sound was sharper than he remembered, each step feeling louder than the last. He wasn't sure where to begin. Should he start with the dusting? The windows? Or was it the old furniture that needed to be dealt with first? Everything seemed overwhelming, each task like a reminder of the past that had led him to this moment.

Grace, standing just behind him in the doorway, broke the silence. "I could help," she said quietly, her voice soft but sure. She had already taken a step inside, but she kept her distance, unsure of how far she was allowed to go in this space that had once been so intimate.

Ethan glanced at her, his chest tightening. He hadn't expected her to offer, hadn't expected her to even be here. The last time they'd spoken, it had been years—years since he'd run away from everything, from her. Yet, here she was, standing in the very room where their story had started, and she was offering to help.

For a moment, he said nothing. He wasn't sure what to say, or if he even wanted help. But then, there was something in her eyes—an unspoken understanding, a quiet willingness to be there for him in a way that no one else had been. And that was Grace. Always steady, always there, even when he didn't deserve it.

He nodded, almost imperceptibly. "Alright. I could use some help."

It wasn't much of a reply, but it was enough.

They moved through the house together, each of them silently choosing a task to focus on. Ethan began with the living room, wiping down the surfaces, the familiar movements of his childhood coming back to him. His hands worked mechanically, the motion almost soothing in its repetition. But as the dust settled, so did the weight of the house's history, the memories of what had once been.

Grace busied herself in the kitchen, cleaning out old cupboards, pulling out forgotten dishes and cups, some chipped, some cracked. They didn't speak much as they worked. It wasn't necessary. There was something in the air between them, a quiet tension, a recognition of the distance that had grown over the years, yet also something unspoken—something still tethering them together.

Ethan could hear the sound of her moving around the kitchen, the quiet rustle of her hands on the counter, the soft clink of dishes being placed into the sink. He found himself drawn to the sounds, a reminder of the comfort she had once provided. But he couldn't shake the feeling that, no matter how much time had passed, they were still two people living in different worlds now.

A creak of the floorboards interrupted his thoughts. Grace had entered the living room, her arms full of things she'd found in the kitchen. She set them down on the table in front of him, her eyes meeting his briefly before she spoke.

"I found these," she said, her voice quiet. "I thought you might want to go through them."

Ethan looked down at the items she had gathered—an old photo album, a collection of letters, and a few of his mother's old trinkets. It was strange, seeing all these things again. He hadn't thought about them in years. He hadn't wanted to.

But now, with Grace standing there, offering him the past, it felt... different. It felt like a lifeline thrown his way, an invitation to step back into the person he had been before he'd left Ashville. And that terrified him.

He picked up the photo album first, his fingers hesitating as he opened it. The first page was filled with pictures of his mother, his father—smiling faces from a time when things had seemed simpler. But the further he turned the pages, the more distant the memories became, like they belonged to someone else. And then, there it was. A photo of him, young, before the world had turned on its axis. And beside him, in the corner of the photo, was Grace—her smile as bright as it had always been, her eyes filled with something more.

His heart stuttered in his chest.

"I never meant to leave you," he whispered, the words slipping out before he could stop them.

Grace didn't respond at first. She simply stood there, her gaze soft as she watched him, waiting for him to continue, to say the words that had been left unsaid for so long.

"I didn't think it would matter," he added, more to himself than to her. "But it does, doesn't it?"

Grace nodded, her voice gentle. "It always mattered, Ethan."

Ethan stood in the kitchen, the air thick with the dust of a house long left neglected. The faded walls seemed to hold a thousand memories, each one a reminder of a life he had tried to outrun. He'd expected the house to feel like a prison, but instead, it felt like a relic—something that belonged to another version of himself, a version he wasn't sure he even recognized anymore.

The task before him was simple but monumental. There was so much to do before this place could be sold: repainting the walls, fixing broken fixtures, mowing the overgrown lawn, and cleaning out every last bit of the old life his father had left behind. Every room, every corner, every inch of this place had been touched by the hands of a man Ethan had tried so hard to forget. And now, it was his responsibility to make it presentable, to let go of the past, and turn this house into something new.

He glanced out the window. The yard was overgrown, the grass swaying in the breeze like an unruly garden of thorns. The bushes in front had long since taken over, and there were cracked tiles leading up to the front porch. He couldn't help but wonder how it had all been allowed to fall into such disrepair. His mother would've never let it get this bad.

With a heavy sigh, he grabbed the rake and started clearing the yard. The rhythmic sound of the rake scraping against the ground helped settle his thoughts, but it didn't take away the feeling of being stuck—stuck in this town, stuck in this house, stuck in his own past.

He worked in silence for a while, lost in the tedious tasks that felt like the only things that would help him avoid thinking too much. But as the sun dipped lower in the sky, the quiet was broken by the sound of his phone vibrating in his pocket. He stopped for a moment, wiping his hands on his jeans before pulling it out.

The name on the screen made him pause: **Clara.**

With a resigned sigh, he answered. "Clara, hey."

"Ethan! How's it going? You getting everything sorted?"

Ethan leaned back against the rake and stared out at the yard. "Not as fast as I'd like. It's going to take a little longer than expected."

He could hear the concern in her voice. "What do you mean? Is everything okay?"

He hesitated. "It's just... a lot of work, you know? The place is in worse shape than I thought. I need to repaint, clean, fix the yard. It's going to be another few days, maybe even longer. I'm sorry."

There was a pause on the other end of the line before Clara spoke again, her voice softer. "I know how you are, Ethan. You're a perfectionist, trying to make everything perfect before you leave. But just remember, you're not doing this alone. You've got people there for you, okay?"

Ethan could feel the weight of her words. She was right. He wasn't doing this alone. But he hadn't let anyone truly in for so long, and it was harder than he expected to even think about accepting help.

"I know. I'll get it done," he said, more to reassure himself than Clara.

There was a brief pause before Clara spoke again. "Okay, well, just let me know if you need anything. Don't overdo it. And remember to eat. I'll take care of the shop while you're away, just focus on what you need to do there."

Ethan chuckled softly, appreciating her no-nonsense approach. "I'll be fine. Thanks, Clara."

They exchanged a few more words before he hung up, and just as he was about to return to the yard, he heard a light knock on the door. He straightened, wiping his hands on his jeans again. For a moment, he stood there, unsure if he was imagining things. But then the door creaked open, and Grace stepped inside.

Her presence was a strange kind of warmth, like sunlight breaking through a storm. Ethan swallowed hard, forcing himself to let go of the fleeting emotions that tugged at his chest. He couldn't let himself go there—not now.

"Is everything okay?" Grace asked, her eyes scanning the room with a quiet intensity.

Ethan nodded, but there was a hint of frustration in his voice. "Just cleaning up. It's going to take a while."

She looked around, noticing the half-painted walls, the bags of trash by the door, and the way the house felt like it was falling apart at the seams. "I can help," she said simply, as though it was the most natural thing in the world.

Ethan opened his mouth to refuse, but something in the way she stood there—quiet and unassuming—made him hesitate. He hadn't been good at asking for help, but for some reason, he didn't want to turn her away.

"Maybe just… for today," he said, surprising even himself with his willingness to accept the offer.

Grace smiled softly, that same gentle, understanding smile he remembered so well. "I'm here if you need me," she said. "What do you want me to do first?"

Ethan paused for a moment, then gestured toward the stack of cleaning supplies in the corner. "You could help with the windows. There's a lot to clean."

She nodded and immediately went to work, and they fell into a quiet rhythm—working side by side, the kind of quiet companionship they'd shared all those years ago. It wasn't perfect, but for the first time in a long time, Ethan didn't feel so alone.

As the afternoon faded into evening, the weight of the house—and the weight of everything it represented—seemed to lessen, just a little.

"I haven't been here in years," Grace said suddenly, breaking the silence.

Ethan glanced up from the window he was wiping down. "Yeah. I didn't think I'd ever come back."

There was a moment of quiet between them, and then Grace smiled faintly. "It's funny, isn't it? How time changes everything, but also nothing at all."

Ethan felt a pang of something deep inside, a mixture of guilt and longing. He didn't know what to say to that. He'd spent so many years running from this place—running from her—and now here he was, standing in it, sharing it with her.

He turned away, looking back at the yard through the window. "Yeah," he said quietly. "Funny."

Grace didn't say anything more, but Ethan could feel her gaze on him, like she understood more than he was letting on. The weight of his past was still there, heavy and uncomfortable, but for the first time in a long time, he didn't feel like he was carrying it all alone.

The silence in the house wasn't uncomfortable, but it wasn't completely easy either. It was a quiet that hummed with unspoken words, both of them avoiding the obvious—the elephant in the room that had followed them all these years: the past. The brokenness. The abandonment.

As they worked, they fell into an unspoken rhythm. Grace cleaned the windows, her hands steady and sure, while Ethan worked on the patching the walls and repainting the old furniture. The tasks were menial, but the weight of them felt significant, as if each brushstroke, each swipe of the cloth, was helping them chip away at the time that had passed between them.

"So, how's life been for you?" Ethan asked, glancing over at her as he worked on the doorframe. He hadn't meant to ask, but the words slipped out before he could stop them.

Grace paused, wiping a stray lock of hair behind her ear. Her eyes softened, and she looked at him for a moment, as if trying to decide just how much of herself she should reveal.

"It's been… okay," she said, her voice quiet, thoughtful. "After you left, I stayed here for a while. Took care of my parents. Then I moved into a little house on the other side of town. Nothing too exciting." She smiled lightly, but it was tinged with something—regret, maybe, or a longing for something more than she had allowed herself. "I didn't really know what to do with myself for a while after you were gone. It felt like… I don't know. Like the whole town was just going through the motions, and I was stuck in place."

Ethan watched her, a knot forming in his stomach. He knew all too well the feeling she was talking about. But he couldn't bring himself to say anything. He had left, had chosen to run, and in doing so, had left her behind, stuck in her own kind of limbo.

"I'm sorry, Grace," he said, his voice thick with something he couldn't name. He wasn't sure if he was apologizing for leaving, for not being there, or for the fact that he had no idea how to fix things.

Grace turned to him, her eyes soft and understanding. "Ethan, don't apologize. You did what you had to do. I… I never wanted to be someone who held you back. And besides, we both made choices. You're not the only one who was trying to move on."

Ethan swallowed hard, the weight of her words settling deep inside him. She was right, of course. They had both made choices, both turned away from each other when they needed each other most. But hearing her speak those words—words that held no bitterness—hurt in a way he hadn't expected.

They worked in silence again, the air thick with thoughts that neither of them was brave enough to voice. But as the hours passed, the work on the house slowly started to feel less like a chore and more like a bridge—a bridge between the past and whatever it was they were building now.

Later, when the sun had begun to set, casting a warm golden light over the room, Grace paused in her cleaning. She looked over at Ethan, her eyes searching his face like she was trying to see the person he had become, the person who had left and never looked back.

"Do you ever think about leaving again?" she asked, the question slipping out before she could stop herself.

Ethan froze, the brush in his hand suddenly feeling like it weighed a ton. He didn't want to think about it. Didn't want to acknowledge the truth that lingered at the back of his mind—that this was temporary. That he would leave again, just like he always had.

But he couldn't lie to her. Not now.

"Yeah," he admitted quietly, his voice heavy. "I think about it all the time."

Grace didn't look surprised, but her expression faltered. "I thought maybe… you'd changed. I thought maybe you'd stayed because of this." She waved her hand toward the house, toward the work they had done together, toward the bond that seemed to be forming between them again.

Ethan looked down at his hands, feeling a sense of guilt gnawing at him. "I haven't changed as much as I'd like to think," he said, his voice low. "I came back because I had to, Grace. The house, the estate… it was all unfinished business. But I'm not staying."

Grace's shoulders slumped, just slightly. "I get it. I really do. But… I just thought, maybe for once, you could stay. For real."

Ethan let out a deep breath, feeling the weight of her words settle over him. He wanted to stay. He wanted to believe that this place, this moment, could be enough to erase the years of running. He wanted to believe that he could settle here, with her, and leave the past behind.

But he couldn't. Not yet.

"I can't, Grace," he said, his voice breaking slightly. "I've built a life now, a whole different life. I'm not that person anymore. I'm not the kid who ran from here. I'm someone else."

She looked at him for a long moment, her gaze filled with a sadness he hadn't expected. "Maybe you're right. Maybe you are someone else. But that doesn't mean you have to leave everything behind."

Ethan shook his head, the words feeling too heavy in his mouth. "It's not that simple. I can't just… stay. I have responsibilities. People who depend on me."

The silence between them stretched out, thick and uncomfortable. He could see the hurt in Grace's eyes, the same hurt he'd left behind all those years ago. But this time, he didn't have an answer for her. Not one that would make things better.

After a long moment, Grace spoke again, her voice quiet but firm. "I won't ask you to stay, Ethan. But I think… I think you should think about it. Really think about it. What are you running from now?"

Ethan looked away, focusing on the half-finished task before him. He didn't want to face the question. He wasn't sure if he could.

But somewhere deep inside, he knew she was right. He'd been running for so long, from everything, from everyone, including himself. And maybe, just maybe, it was time to stop.

The following afternoon, with the house's major cleaning tasks temporarily paused, Grace convinced Ethan to take a walk through town. It wasn't so much a suggestion as a determined insistence, her bright tone cutting through his quiet resistance.

"You've been cooped up in that house for days," she said, handing him his jacket. "You might as well see what's changed since you left."

Ethan had little energy to argue, so he followed her out into the crisp air. The town was quieter than he remembered, the streets less crowded than they had been in his youth. Ashville felt smaller now, like a postcard version of the place he once called home. The storefronts were familiar but faded, some marked by time, others reinvented into something entirely new.

Grace walked beside him, her hands tucked into her coat pockets. She led him down the main street, her steps easy and confident.

"See that?" she said, pointing toward a small café on the corner. The awning was a vibrant green, and the sign above the door read "Sugar Maple Café." "That used to be Ben's Hardware. It's a café now. Best coffee in town—although that's not saying much."

Ethan raised an eyebrow. "Ben's Hardware? Didn't that place have, like, ten aisles of nails and not much else?"

Grace laughed, a sound that felt lighter than it had in days. "Exactly. The café's an upgrade, trust me."

They continued down the street, Grace pointing out the small changes—new businesses, fresh coats of paint on old signs, a mural someone had painted on the side of the community center. Each observation carried a sense of pride, her voice tinged with a fondness that Ethan couldn't quite understand.

"And over there," she said, nodding toward a playground tucked behind the library, "is where we used to hang out after school. They replaced the old swing set with that monstrosity of a jungle gym, but the big oak tree is still there."

Ethan followed her gaze, a wave of nostalgia washing over him. The oak tree stood tall and steady, its branches reaching toward the sky. He could still remember the hours they spent there, trading stories and secrets, escaping the weight of the world even if just for a little while.

"Looks like it's held up better than I have," he muttered.

Grace glanced at him, her expression softening. "You've held up just fine, Ethan."

He didn't respond, instead letting his gaze linger on the playground, on the faint echoes of laughter that seemed to linger in the air. It felt surreal, standing here again, so close to the life he had left behind.

They wandered farther, past the high school, which looked smaller than he remembered, and the old diner where they used to grab milkshakes after football games. Grace didn't rush him, letting the memories come and go at their own pace.

Eventually, they reached the edge of town, where the fields stretched out toward the horizon. The golden light of the setting sun bathed everything in a warm glow, and for a moment, the weight on Ethan's chest seemed to lift.

"It's strange," he said quietly, breaking the silence. "Being back here. It's like… nothing's changed, but everything has."

Grace nodded, her gaze fixed on the horizon. "That's how it goes, isn't it? Life keeps moving, even when you're not here to see it."

Ethan glanced at her, the sunlight catching the edges of her hair, making it glow. "What about you? Has life been moving for you, Grace? Or does it still feel like you're stuck?"

She turned to him, her expression unreadable. "Sometimes it feels like I'm stuck," she admitted. "But then I look around, and I see how much has changed. And I realize it's not the town that's holding me back. It's me."

Her honesty struck a chord in him, and for a moment, he wasn't sure what to say. Grace had always been good at cutting to the heart of things, at saying what he didn't have the courage to.

"You're not stuck," he said finally, his voice firm. "You're... steady. There's a difference."

She gave him a small smile, but it didn't quite reach her eyes. "And you're still running."

Her words hit him harder than he expected, and he looked away, his gaze falling on the fields. She wasn't wrong, but hearing her say it out loud made it harder to ignore.

They stood there for a while, the silence between them filled with unspoken thoughts. Ethan wasn't sure how long they stayed like that, watching the sun dip lower and lower, but for the first time in a long time, he didn't feel the need to run.

Eventually, Grace broke the silence. "Come on," she said, her voice lightening. "I know a place that still makes the best apple pie you've ever tasted. My treat."

Ethan hesitated for a moment before following her back toward town. As they walked, he felt something shift—something small but significant. It wasn't forgiveness, not yet, but it was a step toward something he couldn't quite name.

And for now, that was enough.

The next few days followed a rhythm Ethan hadn't expected, one of unspoken truce and tentative rebuilding. Grace was at the house more often than not, her presence a constant that somehow felt less intrusive and more necessary with each passing moment. While Ethan focused on the endless tasks to get the house ready for sale—painting walls, patching broken floorboards, clearing out debris—Grace became an anchor, helping him without being asked, filling the silence with her voice.

Sometimes they worked in companionable quiet; other times, their conversations drifted into deeper waters, each word dredging up pieces of the past that neither of them had fully let go of.

One morning, as sunlight streamed through the kitchen windows, Grace stood at the counter, wiping down the faded tiles. Ethan was perched on a ladder nearby, carefully painting the trim. The smell of fresh paint mixed with the scent of coffee Grace had brewed earlier, a strange but comforting blend.

"You remember the summer of the storm?" Grace asked suddenly, her voice soft.

Ethan paused, his brush hovering midair. "The storm?"

She turned, leaning against the counter. "Yeah. The one that knocked out power for three days. We spent the whole time hiding out in your mom's living room, eating all the snacks she let us raid from the pantry."

Ethan chuckled, the memory tugging at the corners of his mouth. "And playing cards by candlelight until we couldn't see straight."

Grace's smile grew, but there was a wistfulness in her eyes. "Your mom was the only one in town who wasn't worried about the storm. She just kept saying, 'The worst storms don't last forever.' I think she meant more than just the weather."

Ethan swallowed, the warmth of the memory clashing with the cold reality of everything that followed. "She always knew how to make things feel... safe."

Grace nodded, her gaze falling to the floor. "She was the best part of this town. I think losing her was the first time I really understood what it meant to lose something."

Ethan's chest tightened, and he forced himself to keep painting, to focus on the repetitive motion instead of the emotions threatening to surface. "I lost more than just her that year."

Grace looked up at him, her expression unreadable. "I know."

For a moment, neither of them spoke. The weight of their shared history hung in the air, heavy and unyielding.

That afternoon, Grace suggested they take another break, insisting that even Ethan needed to breathe. She led him down an old dirt path behind the house, one that snaked through the woods and eventually opened into a small clearing.

The space was overgrown now, the grass tall and wildflowers dotting the landscape, but Ethan recognized it instantly. It was their place, the spot they used to escape to when the world felt too big and their lives too complicated.

"I can't believe this is still here," Ethan murmured, stepping into the clearing.

Grace smiled faintly. "Not everything changes."

He walked to the center, turning slowly to take it all in. The tree they used to climb was still standing, its branches reaching out like old friends. He could almost see their younger selves, sprawled out on the grass, dreaming about futures they couldn't yet imagine.

"We used to talk about running away," he said, his voice quieter now. "You said you wanted to go to the city, see the world."

Grace laughed softly, the sound tinged with irony. "And you actually did it."

"Yeah," Ethan said, his gaze distant. "But it didn't feel the way we thought it would."

She tilted her head, studying him. "What did it feel like?"

Ethan hesitated, searching for the right words. "Like I left something behind. Something I didn't even realize I needed until it was too late."

Grace's breath caught, but she recovered quickly, her expression carefully neutral. "You had to leave, Ethan. I understood that then, and I understand it now."

"But you didn't deserve to be left like that," he said, meeting her gaze. "You were the only good thing I had, Grace, and I just... I threw it all away."

She shook her head, her smile sad but steady. "You didn't throw it away. You just didn't know how to hold onto it."

Ethan's throat tightened, and for a moment, he thought he might fall apart right there in the clearing. But Grace's presence grounded him, just like it always had.

Over the next few days, their conversations grew longer, their silences more comfortable. Grace opened up about her life in Ashville—how she had stayed because it felt like the only thing she could do, how she had found joy in small things, even when the weight of the town threatened to crush her.

Ethan shared pieces of his own journey, though he kept most of the darker parts to himself. He told her about the people who had helped him, about the life he had built, about the moments of success that felt hollow without anyone to share them with.

They fell into an easy rhythm, their conversations laced with the kind of honesty that only came from years of knowing someone. The walls between them began to crumble, piece by piece, until the possibility of something more started to feel less like a distant dream and more like a fragile reality.

But beneath it all, the unspoken truth lingered: Ethan couldn't stay. And Grace wouldn't leave.

Ethan leaned against the counter, his arms crossed, watching as Grace placed the dishes carefully back into the cabinet. The sunlight filtered through the window, casting a soft glow around her, and for a fleeting moment, the scene felt almost normal. Almost like the life he'd sometimes imagined but never dared to hope for.

"You've always been good at organizing," Ethan said, breaking the comfortable silence.

Grace turned, holding a chipped mug with faded flowers painted on its surface. She smiled softly. "And you've always been good at making messes for me to organize."

A chuckle escaped him. "Fair point."

They worked together, clearing out the remnants of a past life one room at a time. The rhythm of their efforts felt strangely therapeutic, even as the weight of the house pressed down on them. Every creak of the floorboards seemed to whisper memories neither of them were ready to fully confront.

As Ethan moved to the hall closet, he hesitated. The small space held his mother's old things—he hadn't dared to open it before. But with Grace nearby, he felt a little braver.

Inside, he found a faded shoebox labeled "Mom's Keepsakes." He carried it to the living room and set it on the coffee table, calling Grace over.

"What's that?" she asked, sitting cross-legged on the floor beside him.

"Stuff she kept," Ethan said, his voice quieter than he intended. "I haven't opened it since—" He stopped, swallowing hard.

Grace placed a comforting hand on his knee. "You don't have to do this now if you're not ready."

He shook his head. "No. I want to."

As they sifted through the box, Ethan found small treasures: old photographs, letters, and a locket that held a picture of his mother and him as a baby. Grace studied the items with quiet reverence, letting Ethan take the lead.

"She always wore this," Ethan murmured, holding up the locket.

"I remember," Grace said, her voice tinged with nostalgia. "She used to say it was her way of keeping you close, even when you were running off with your friends."

Ethan laughed lightly, though the sound carried a trace of sadness. "She deserved so much better than this place. Than him."

The mood shifted as Ethan uncovered something else at the bottom of the box: an empty whiskey bottle, hidden beneath the keepsakes. The sight of it hit him like a punch to the gut.

He froze, the memories rushing back with a cruel clarity. His father's slurred words. The crashes of bottles against walls. The way his mother would shield him, even as she bore the brunt of the anger.

Grace noticed his change in demeanor. "Ethan?"

He held up the bottle, his jaw tightening. "He couldn't go a day without one of these. I thought I'd thrown them all out, but… I guess not."

Grace reached for his hand, her fingers intertwining with his. "It wasn't your fault. None of it."

"I know that," he said, though his voice wavered. "But it still feels like it. Sometimes, I wonder if leaving was the right thing. If I'd stayed, maybe I could've—"

"No," Grace interrupted firmly. "You did what you had to do to survive. Staying wouldn't have changed him, Ethan. It might've broken you, too."

Her words settled in the air between them, heavy but true. Ethan stared at the bottle for a moment longer before setting it down with finality.

"Let's get back to work," he said, his voice steadier now.

Grace nodded, understanding his need to move forward. They spent the next hour sorting through more of his mother's belongings, sharing stories and memories that painted a picture of the woman she had been.

By the time the sun dipped below the horizon, the house felt lighter—not in the physical sense, but in the way the past seemed a little less overwhelming.

Ethan glanced at Grace as they packed up for the evening. "Thanks for being here," he said softly.

"Always," she replied, her smile warm and unwavering.

And for the first time in years, Ethan felt a glimmer of something he thought he'd lost forever: hope.

The evening brought a stillness to the house, the kind that came with the quiet settling of dust and the faint hum of cicadas outside. Ethan stood at the window in what used to be the living room, staring out at the overgrown yard. Grace had gone to the kitchen to start a pot of tea, leaving him alone with his thoughts.

His gaze drifted to the treehouse at the edge of the property, its frame barely visible in the twilight. He'd forgotten it was there, hidden behind the tangle of branches and neglect.

"Did you build that with your dad?" Grace's voice broke the silence as she entered the room, two steaming mugs in her hands.

Ethan turned, accepting a mug with a quiet "Thanks." He took a sip, the warmth settling in his chest. "No. My mom helped me build it. Said every kid needed a place to escape."

Grace smiled faintly. "I remember when you showed it to me. You said it was your kingdom, and I was your most trusted knight."

Ethan chuckled, the memory tugging at a corner of his mouth. "Yeah, and you kept trying to convince me to let you be the queen instead."

"I was ahead of my time," Grace teased, her eyes twinkling.

They stood there in comfortable silence for a moment, the past weaving its way between them. Grace leaned against the wall, her mug cradled in her hands. "Why don't you fix it up? The treehouse, I mean. It could be… I don't know, a way to honor her."

Ethan tilted his head, considering the idea. "Maybe," he said after a pause. "But I'm not sure I'm ready for that yet."

Grace nodded, understanding. She glanced around the room. "You've made a lot of progress here today. The place is starting to feel less... haunted."

"Still feels haunted to me," Ethan muttered, his voice low.

Grace placed her mug on the windowsill and stepped closer to him. "Maybe it's not the house that's haunted. Maybe it's you."

Her words weren't accusatory—they were gentle, spoken with the kind of honesty only Grace could deliver. Ethan didn't reply, but the weight of her observation settled heavily in his chest.

They spent the next hour sorting through another box of his mother's belongings. Most of it was old linens, but beneath it all, Ethan found a small leather journal. The cover was worn, the pages yellowed with age. He opened it carefully, his breath catching as he recognized his mother's handwriting.

"It's hers," he said, his voice barely above a whisper.

Grace moved closer, peering over his shoulder. "What does it say?"

Ethan flipped through the pages, scanning fragments of entries. They were simple, everyday notes—grocery lists, reminders to pay bills—but interspersed were little snippets of thoughts.

Ethan had a rough day at school. Wish I could do more to help him feel better.

Made his favorite cookies today. He said they were too burnt, but he ate three anyway.

I'm so proud of the man he's becoming. I hope he knows how much I love him, even if I don't say it enough.

The words hit Ethan like a tidal wave. He hadn't realized how much he needed to hear her voice again, even if it was only through ink on paper.

Grace placed a hand on his arm, grounding him. "She loved you so much, Ethan."

He nodded, swallowing hard. "I know. I just... I wish I could've done more for her. Given her a better life."

"You gave her the one thing that mattered most," Grace said softly. "You."

Ethan closed the journal, holding it tightly. He didn't have the words to respond, but Grace's presence said enough.

They worked until late into the night, the house slowly shedding its layers of sorrow. And when they finally called it a day, Ethan felt something he hadn't felt in years: the faintest flicker of peace.

As they prepared to leave, Ethan lingered by the door. His gaze swept over the room, taking in the progress they'd made. "Thanks for helping me today," he said, his voice steady.

Grace smiled, her hand brushing lightly against his. "You don't have to thank me, Ethan. I'm here because I want to be."

Her words stayed with him long after she'd gone, echoing in the stillness of the night.

The next morning, Ethan stood in the dining room, staring at a crooked picture frame that hung stubbornly on the wall. It was one of the few things left untouched during the whirlwind of cleaning and repairs. The photo inside was faded, the colors muted with time, but the image was unmistakable: a family portrait from when he was just a kid.

His mother was seated in the middle, her warm smile a beacon of love. His father stood stiffly beside her, a hand resting on her shoulder. Ethan was in the front, maybe six or seven years old, his expression a mixture of boyish mischief and innocence.

He reached out, his fingers brushing against the glass. It felt like a lifetime ago—like another boy, another family, another world.

"You okay?" Grace's voice came from behind him.

Ethan glanced over his shoulder, offering a half-hearted smile. "Yeah. Just... trying to decide if I should leave this up or pack it away."

Grace stepped closer, studying the photo. "You look so much like her."

He nodded, his throat tightening. "She used to say that, too. Always said I had her smile."

Grace smiled softly. "She wasn't wrong."

Ethan took the frame off the wall, holding it in his hands. "I think I'll keep it. Not here, though. Somewhere else. Somewhere it doesn't feel so heavy."

Grace didn't press further, sensing the weight of the moment. Instead, she gestured toward the kitchen. "Come on, I made coffee. Figured we'd need it for the yard work."

Ethan followed her, setting the picture frame gently on the counter before grabbing a mug. They sat at the kitchen table, the early morning sunlight streaming through the windows.

"So, what's the plan for today?" Grace asked, wrapping her hands around her cup.

Ethan leaned back in his chair, running a hand through his hair. "Yard's the big one. Needs mowing, trimming, maybe even some weeding. I also need to check the gutters and make sure the roof's still in good shape.

The realtor will probably suggest some landscaping, but I'll leave that decision for later."

Grace nodded thoughtfully. "Sounds like a lot. You sure you don't want some help?"

Ethan raised an eyebrow. "You volunteering to push a lawn mower?"

She laughed, rolling her eyes. "Maybe not that, but I can weed with the best of them."

"Deal," he said with a grin.

They spent the morning tackling the yard, the sun climbing higher as the hours passed. Grace worked on the flowerbeds, pulling out stubborn weeds and clearing away debris, while Ethan handled the mowing and trimming. The rhythmic hum of the mower and the occasional rustle of leaves filled the air, a soothing soundtrack to their labor.

When they paused for lunch, they sat on the front porch, their arms and clothes smudged with dirt. Grace handed Ethan a sandwich she'd packed earlier, and they ate in companionable silence.

"This place doesn't look half bad," Grace said, glancing at the freshly mowed lawn and tidied flowerbeds.

"Thanks to you," Ethan replied, taking a sip of water.

She shrugged, smiling. "Team effort."

After lunch, they tackled the gutters and roof, discovering that years of neglect had left their mark. There were leaves and twigs clogging the gutters, and a few shingles that needed replacing.

As they worked, Ethan found himself sharing more about his life in Gulf City—how he'd built the furniture repair business from the ground up, how Clara had been the first person to give him a chance, and how he'd finally found a place that felt like his own.

Grace listened intently, asking questions and laughing at his stories about the eccentric customers and chaotic early days of the shop.

"I'm glad you found your way," she said as they climbed down from the roof. "I always knew you would. You're too stubborn to give up."

Ethan chuckled. "Yeah, well, stubbornness only gets you so far. Sometimes, it's the people who believe in you that make the difference."

Their eyes met, and for a moment, the weight of their shared history hung between them.

"You've always had people who believed in you, Ethan," Grace said softly.

He nodded, his gaze dropping to the ground. "Yeah. I just wish I hadn't taken them for granted."

The rest of the afternoon was spent finishing the last of the yard work and tidying up the garage. By the time they called it a day, the house and its surroundings looked almost unrecognizable—like a place that had been cared for, loved even.

As they stood on the porch, surveying their work, Ethan let out a long breath. "Thanks for today. I couldn't have done this without you."

Grace smiled, nudging him lightly with her shoulder. "You've said that before. You know you don't have to thank me, right?"

"Maybe," he said, his voice quiet. "But I still want to."

Grace held his gaze, her expression softening. "You're welcome, Ethan."

The moment stretched between them, charged with something unspoken. But before either of them could say more, the distant sound of crickets and the fading light reminded them of the day's end.

"Same time tomorrow?" Grace asked, breaking the silence.

Ethan smiled faintly. "Yeah. Same time."

She gave him a small wave as she walked down the driveway, leaving him alone with the house and his thoughts once more.

As the sun dipped below the horizon, casting the sky in deep shades of orange and purple, Ethan remained on the porch, staring out at the quiet street. The day's work had left him physically exhausted but mentally restless. His hands were calloused and dirty, but his thoughts were raw and tangled.

He stepped back inside, the house now eerily quiet. The faint scent of fresh-cut grass and turned soil clung to his clothes as he wandered through the living room, his gaze skimming over the freshly cleaned surfaces and repaired furniture.

In the dim light, he caught sight of a box pushed into the corner. He didn't remember seeing it earlier, and curiosity pulled him toward it. He knelt, tugging it open to reveal its contents: stacks of his mother's things. Old photo albums, a collection of recipes written in her elegant handwriting, and a small wooden jewelry box.

Ethan hesitated before opening the jewelry box. Inside, he found a delicate gold necklace with a tiny heart-shaped pendant—his mother's favorite. He held it up, the metal catching the faint light. A wave of emotion hit him like a freight train, memories of her laughter and warmth flooding his mind.

He slipped the necklace into his pocket, unsure why but unable to leave it behind.

Digging further into the box, his hand brushed against a collection of folded papers. He pulled them out and unfolded one, instantly recognizing his mother's handwriting. It was a letter addressed to him.

Ethan froze, his breath catching in his throat.

Dear Ethan,

If you're reading this, it means I'm no longer there to tell you these things myself. I wish I could have stayed longer, been there to see the man you would grow up to be. But if there's one thing I know, it's that you were always destined for something bigger than this town, bigger than anything I could imagine.

I hope you never forget how proud I am of you, how much I loved you, even when things were hard. You have your whole life ahead of you, Ethan. Don't let the darkness of this place hold you back. Find your light, your purpose, and never stop chasing it.

Love always,
 Mom

Ethan's vision blurred as he read the letter, his mother's words cutting through the walls he'd built around his emotions. He pressed the letter to his chest, closing his eyes as a deep ache settled in his heart.

It took him a long moment to compose himself. Carefully, he folded the letter and placed it back in the box, setting it aside to take with him.

He rose to his feet, heading upstairs to the bedroom. There was still work to be done tomorrow, but for now, he needed to rest.

As he lay in bed, staring up at the cracked ceiling, his mind wandered back to Grace. Her laughter, her kindness, the way she seemed to anchor him in a way no one else ever had.

But even as he thought about her, another thought crept in, one he couldn't shake: this was temporary. The house, the town, Grace—they were all part of a past he'd left behind. His life was in Gulf City now, with Clara, Joe, and Maria, with the business he'd worked so hard to build.

And yet, lying there in the quiet of the night, Ethan couldn't deny the tug of something deeper. Something he wasn't ready to name.

Tomorrow would come, and with it, more time with Grace, more memories unearthed, more questions he didn't have answers to. For now, though, he let the weight of the day pull him into sleep, the faint echo of his mother's words and Grace's smile lingering in the edges of his dreams.

The morning sunlight filtered through the freshly cleaned windows, casting warm beams of light onto the newly polished wooden floors. The house was almost unrecognizable now—a far cry from the decaying monument to Ethan's past it had been just days ago. The walls were repainted, the floors scrubbed and refinished, and the broken fixtures replaced. Every inch of the house bore the mark of Ethan's labor, but it wasn't just his hands that had transformed it. Grace's touch was everywhere too, from the curtains she'd insisted on hanging to the way she'd arranged the furniture.

Ethan stood in the middle of the living room, his hands on his hips, surveying the finished work. He couldn't deny the pang of pride he felt, but it was bittersweet. This wasn't his home. It had never truly been.

Grace appeared in the doorway, her sleeves rolled up and a smudge of paint on her cheek. "Well, Blackwell," she said with a smile, "I think we did it. The place looks... livable."

Ethan chuckled, the sound coming out lighter than he expected. "It looks more than livable. It looks like a home."

Grace tilted her head, studying him for a moment. "Do you think it'll sell?"

He nodded slowly. "Yeah, someone will want it. It's a good house... now."

A quiet settled between them, the kind that had grown increasingly comfortable over the past few days. Grace leaned against the doorframe, watching him with that curious, thoughtful expression she always seemed to have around him.

"You've changed," she said softly, breaking the silence.

Ethan looked at her, startled by the statement. "What do you mean?"

"I mean... you're different. The Ethan I knew would've never come back to this house, let alone cleaned it up and made it look like this. You've grown, in ways I didn't think were possible back then."

He felt a lump form in his throat, her words hitting something raw inside him. "I didn't have much of a choice," he admitted. "I had to change. If I didn't... I don't know if I'd have made it."

Grace took a step closer, her eyes never leaving his. "But you did make it. You left, and you built something for yourself. That's no small thing."

Ethan swallowed hard, his chest tightening. "And you stayed. You stayed, and you built a life here."

She shrugged, a faint smile on her lips. "It's not always easy, but it's my home. And I've found my place in it."

Their gazes locked, the air between them charged with an emotion neither of them dared to name. Ethan felt his walls cracking, the ones he'd spent years building to keep his feelings buried.

"Grace..." he started, his voice barely above a whisper.

She stepped even closer, closing the distance between them. "Ethan, I know this is temporary for you. I know you're going to leave again, and I've told myself I'm okay with that. But right now, in this moment, I need to know—did any part of you miss this? Miss us?"

The question hit him like a freight train. His heart thudded in his chest, and he struggled to find the words.

"I missed you," he admitted finally, his voice thick with emotion. "Every day, Grace. I missed you so much it hurt."

Her breath hitched, and for a moment, neither of them moved. Then, as if drawn by some invisible force, Ethan closed the distance between them, his hands cupping her face as he kissed her.

It was everything he remembered and more—soft, warm, and filled with a longing that had only grown stronger over the years. Grace melted into him, her hands clutching the front of his shirt as if afraid he might disappear.

When they finally pulled apart, their foreheads rested together, both of them breathing hard.

"I don't want to lose this," Grace said, her voice trembling.

Ethan's chest ached at her words, knowing he was going to break her heart. "I don't either," he whispered, his voice barely audible.

But the unspoken truth hung heavy between them: this was temporary. No matter how much he wanted to stay, no matter how much he wanted to make this work, his life was in Gulf City.

For now, though, he let himself hold her, let himself believe, if only for a moment, that they could rewrite the ending to their story.

Chapter Five

Ethan stood in the kitchen, the freshly cleaned counters gleaming under the soft morning light streaming through the window. His phone rested on the table, the screen displaying the real estate agent's number. He hesitated, his finger hovering over the call button.

The house looked different now—no longer a husk of memories he had once avoided at all costs. But no matter how polished it appeared, the shadows of his father's fury and his mother's quiet strength clung to the corners. It wasn't a home to him; it never had been. It was a reminder.

He finally pressed the button, lifting the phone to his ear. The agent's cheerful voice answered on the second ring, pulling him from his thoughts.

"Mr. Blackwell! How can I help you today?"

"I'm ready," he said, his voice firmer than he felt. "The house—it's ready to be listed. Let's get it on the market."

After hashing out the details, Ethan hung up and leaned against the counter, staring at the sunlight pooling on the floor. It was done. The house would soon belong to someone else, and with it, every tie to Ashville he had tried so hard to sever.

But not every tie.

Grace knocked on the door mid-morning, carrying a basket of muffins she had baked that morning. When Ethan opened the door, her smile was tentative, like she wasn't quite sure where they stood after everything.

"You're still here," she said, holding out the basket. "Figured you might need some breakfast."

He smirked, taking the basket. "You trying to butter me up?"

"Just being neighborly," she said with a shrug. But her eyes held a flicker of something deeper—an unspoken question of whether he was really planning to leave her behind again.

They sat on the back porch, eating in companionable silence, the morning air crisp and alive with the sounds of birds and rustling leaves.

"Things have changed around here," she said, breaking the quiet. "But some things... not so much."

Ethan looked at her, raising an eyebrow. "Like what?"

Grace gestured to the yard. "This tree, for one. We used to climb it, remember? You always dared me to go higher, even though I was terrified."

He chuckled. "And you always called me an idiot when I did."

"Still do," she teased, her smile softening. "But you were fearless, Ethan. At least, that's how it seemed to me."

"Fearless or stupid. Probably a mix of both." He glanced at the tree, a wistful look crossing his face. "I think that's what made leaving so easy. I wasn't thinking about anything other than getting out."

Grace's expression shifted, and for a moment, he thought she might ask the question he dreaded—why he never reached out, never said goodbye. But she didn't. Instead, she picked a piece of grass from the ground and twirled it between her fingers.

"Well," she said, her voice light but her tone serious, "at least you came back."

That afternoon, Grace insisted on showing him around. She took him to the new coffee shop that had replaced the old hardware store, to the renovated library, and even to the park where they used to hang out after school.

They paused at the swings, the metal creaking faintly as the wind pushed them back and forth.

"I used to sit here and wonder where you were," Grace admitted, her gaze fixed on the empty swings. "If you were happy. If you were safe."

Ethan shoved his hands in his pockets, guilt pooling in his chest. "I thought about writing. I even started letters. But I could never bring myself to send them."

Grace looked at him, her expression unreadable. "Why not?"

"I don't know," he admitted, his voice quiet. "Maybe I thought it'd hurt less if I just... disappeared."

"And did it?" she asked, her tone soft but pointed.

He met her gaze, the weight of her question heavy in the air. "No," he said finally. "It didn't."

They ended the day at Grace's house, where she cooked dinner while Ethan helped. The kitchen was small but warm, filled with the smell of roasted vegetables and garlic. They worked side by side, their movements easy and familiar, as if no time had passed.

After dinner, they sat on her porch, watching the fireflies flicker in the fading light.

"Do you think you'll come back?" Grace asked, breaking the quiet.

Ethan hesitated, the truth lodged in his throat. "I don't know," he said finally. "My life... it's in Gulf City now. Everything I've built, everyone who relies on me—it's all there."

Grace nodded, her expression unreadable. "I figured you'd say that."

"But this," he said, gesturing to the town, the house, and her, "it's still a part of me. You're still a part of me."

Her eyes met his, and for a moment, it felt like the years between them didn't exist. But then she looked away, her lips pressing into a faint, bittersweet smile.

"Let's not do this, Ethan," she said softly. "Let's not pretend like this can be anything more than what it is."

Ethan didn't know how to respond, so he didn't. Instead, they sat in silence, the unspoken words hanging between them like the fireflies dotting the darkness.

Ethan woke early, the house quiet around him. For the first time, the silence didn't feel oppressive. Instead, it carried the subtle hum of purpose—the faintest echo of something almost peaceful.

The day stretched ahead, filled with a final checklist of repairs, cleaning, and organizing. He moved through the house methodically, his steps steady, his mind focused. There wasn't much left to do, but each task carried its own weight, as if the house itself was reluctant to let him go.

By late morning, Grace arrived, a bag of sandwiches in hand. She let herself in, calling out, "Don't tell me you've been working all morning without eating."

Ethan appeared from the living room, a hammer in one hand and a half-finished shelf in the other. "I might have," he admitted with a small smirk. "But I'm guessing you'll fix that."

"Damn right I will." She placed the bag on the kitchen table, unpacking the sandwiches and two cold bottles of water. "Sit," she ordered, pointing to the chair.

He obeyed with an exaggerated sigh. "You've gotten bossier over the years."

"I had to, considering how stubborn you are," she shot back, her tone light but her smile soft.

They ate in comfortable silence for a while, the sounds of the old house settling around them.

"So," Grace said finally, breaking the quiet, "how much more is left?"

"Not much," Ethan replied, leaning back in his chair. "A few touch-ups here and there, clearing out the garage. The realtor is coming tomorrow to take pictures."

Grace nodded, her expression thoughtful. "It's really coming together. You've done a good job, Ethan."

"Couldn't have done it without you," he said honestly, his gaze meeting hers.

For a moment, her cheeks flushed, and she looked away. "Well, someone had to make sure you didn't screw it up."

The garage was a mess of half-forgotten tools, rusted nails, and dusty boxes piled in uneven stacks. Ethan and Grace tackled it together, sorting through the remnants of another life.

"Do you think your dad kept anything worth saving in here?" Grace asked, her voice muffled as she dug through a box of old screws.

"Doubt it," Ethan said, opening a battered cabinet. "Most of this is junk he refused to throw away. Just another thing to control, I guess."

As he shifted a box, something clattered to the floor—a heavy, glass bottle. Ethan froze, staring at the whiskey bottle as it rolled to a stop against his boot.

The air grew heavy, the faint scent of aged liquor seeming to seep into the room.

Grace turned at the sound, her expression softening when she saw his face. "Ethan?"

"I thought I got rid of all of these," he said quietly, picking up the bottle. His hand trembled slightly as he turned it over, the label faded but still legible. Memories surged forward—his father's slurred shouts, the sharp crack of a bottle against the wall, the cold fear that settled in his stomach every night as a child.

"Ethan," Grace said again, stepping closer. Her hand brushed his arm, grounding him. "You're not that boy anymore. And he doesn't get to control you now."

He exhaled, his grip tightening on the bottle. "Sometimes it feels like he still does."

Grace reached for the bottle, her touch gentle but firm. "Then let's take that control back."

He hesitated before handing it to her. Together, they carried it outside, where Grace set it on the ground and grabbed a rock. With one swing, she shattered the bottle, the sound sharp and final.

Ethan stared at the shards glinting in the sunlight, his chest tight. "Thanks."

She smiled, her hand finding his again. "Anytime."

As the sun set, the house was nearly finished. The fresh paint gleamed in the soft light, and the yard looked neat and welcoming. It didn't feel like the house Ethan had grown up in—it felt like a blank slate, ready for someone else's story.

Grace sat with him on the front steps, the two of them sharing a quiet moment.

"I think this is the first time I've seen this place look... peaceful," Ethan said, his gaze drifting across the yard.

Grace nodded. "You've done a lot of work—not just on the house."

He looked at her, his brow furrowing. "What do you mean?"

"I mean, you've faced things here that most people would've run from. You're stronger than you think, Ethan."

He didn't know how to respond. Instead, he looked down at his hands, the calluses rough against his skin. "It's funny. I always thought leaving was what made me strong. But now..."

Grace tilted her head, waiting.

"Now I'm not so sure," he admitted.

"You don't have to have all the answers," she said softly. "Sometimes it's enough to just take it one step at a time."

Ethan nodded, her words settling in his chest. He wasn't sure what the next step was, but for the first time in a long time, he wasn't afraid to find out.

The morning broke quiet and still, the kind of stillness that seemed to magnify every sound. Ethan stood at the kitchen counter, pouring himself a cup of coffee. He stared into the dark liquid, his mind already racing with everything he wanted to say and everything he couldn't.

Grace arrived just as the coffee pot clicked off, letting herself in without knocking. She had done so every day since they started working on the house, and it struck him how natural it felt.

"Good morning," she said softly, her smile warm but tinged with something unspoken. She held up a bag of pastries from the local bakery. "Thought we could start the day right."

Ethan smiled back, though it didn't quite reach his eyes. "You always know how to take care of me."

"That's what friends are for," she replied lightly, but the word "friends" hung in the air between them, heavy with meaning.

They ate in comfortable silence, but both seemed to know it wouldn't last.

After breakfast, Grace suggested a walk through town. Ethan agreed, knowing it might be the last time he saw Ashville this way. They strolled down Main Street, past familiar storefronts and new ones that hadn't been there when he left.

"That used to be the diner we'd go to after school," Grace said, pointing to a sleek coffee shop now occupying the space.

Ethan laughed. "I remember. You always ordered the biggest milkshake they had."

"And you always stole half of it," she shot back with a smirk.

They paused outside the old library, its brick façade unchanged. Grace touched the railing, her eyes distant. "Remember when we spent hours in here, pretending to study but just talking about everything and nothing?"

Ethan nodded, the memory vivid in his mind. "You were always better at pretending to study than I was."

They shared a laugh, but it was softer this time, tinged with the weight of everything left unsaid.

They returned to the house as the afternoon sun slanted through the windows. Ethan busied himself tidying up while Grace leaned against the counter, watching him.

"Have you thought about staying?" she asked suddenly.

The question hit him harder than he expected. He froze for a moment, his back to her, before answering. "I can't, Grace. My life... it's back in Gulf City."

She looked down, tracing circles on the counter with her finger. "I know. I just thought maybe—"

"Maybe what?" he asked, turning to face her. His voice was gentle, but the tension was clear.

"Maybe you'd realize this is where you're supposed to be," she said, meeting his gaze. "With me."

The words hung in the air, raw and unfiltered. Ethan didn't know how to respond, so he didn't. Instead, he crossed the room, standing in front of her.

"I wish things were different," he said finally. "But I've built a life there. People depend on me."

"What about me?" Grace whispered, her voice breaking. "Do I matter?"

"You matter more than you know," Ethan said, his voice thick. "That's why this is so hard."

As the sun dipped below the horizon, they sat on the front porch, the silence between them speaking volumes. Grace reached over, her fingers brushing his. "Promise me something?"

"Anything," Ethan said.

"Promise me you'll be happy," she said, her eyes shimmering with unshed tears. "Even if it's not here."

"I'll try," he said, his voice cracking. "But I'm not sure I know how to be happy without you."

Grace smiled faintly, her tears spilling over. "You'll figure it out. You always do."

The sound of a distant train whistle broke the moment, a sharp reminder of what was coming.

"It's time," Ethan said, standing reluctantly.

Grace stood too, wiping her cheeks. "I'll walk you to the station."

They walked side by side, the streets quiet, the air heavy with finality. At the station, Ethan turned to her, his heart pounding.

"Thank you," he said. "For everything. For being here."

Grace nodded, her eyes locked on his. "Goodbye, Ethan."

He hesitated, as if he wanted to say something more, but instead, he simply turned and boarded the train.

As the train pulled away, Ethan sat by the window, watching the town fade into the distance. His bag sat on the seat beside him, the weight of the letters pressing against him like a tangible thing.

Earlier that evening, just before they left for the station, he had slipped out and tucked the bundle of letters into Grace's mailbox. He had left the shoebox behind, but the letters—each one filled with the words he could never say aloud—were now hers.

He didn't know if she would read them, or if she would understand why he hadn't handed them to her directly. But as the train carried him away, he allowed himself the smallest flicker of hope that, someday, they might lead him back to her.

Chapter Six

Ethan walked into the workshop early that morning, the familiar scent of varnish and sawdust wrapping around him like an old coat. The hum of activity hadn't started yet, and for a moment, the silence felt almost sacred. He took a deep breath, letting it steady him as he crossed the floor, his shoes clicking softly against the wood.

He reached his office and paused, the door slightly ajar. Clara sat at his desk, thumbing through a stack of invoices. Her sharp eyes flicked up as he stepped inside, and she leaned back in the chair with a knowing smile.

"You're back earlier than I expected," she said, standing and brushing her hands against her jeans.

"House is done. No reason to linger," Ethan replied, setting his bag down.

Clara studied him for a moment, her arms crossed. "How'd it go?"

"It's taken care of," he said curtly, pulling a file from his desk to avoid her gaze.

"Right," Clara said slowly, her tone skeptical. "And how are you?"

Ethan hesitated, then looked up at her. "I'm fine."

Clara raised an eyebrow. "Liar."

As the day unfolded, Ethan buried himself in work, overseeing projects, checking schedules, and answering emails. But Clara wasn't one to let things slide. By late afternoon, she cornered him in the breakroom, her hands on her hips.

"You've been pacing around like a caged animal all day," she said. "Spill it."

Ethan sighed, leaning against the counter. "It's nothing, Clara. Just getting back into the groove."

"Don't give me that," she said, her tone firm but not unkind. "I've known you long enough to see when something's eating at you. So, what happened in Ashville?"

He hesitated, his jaw tightening. For a moment, he considered brushing her off again, but the weight of everything was too much. "I saw her," he admitted quietly.

Clara blinked. "Her? Grace?"

Ethan nodded, staring at the floor. "She was there. Helping me with the house."

Clara pulled out a chair and sat down, motioning for him to do the same. "And?"

"And... we talked. Worked together. Spent time catching up." He rubbed the back of his neck, his voice heavy. "It felt like nothing had changed, and yet everything had."

"Did you tell her how you feel?" Clara asked.

"I couldn't," Ethan said, his voice barely above a whisper. "What would be the point? My life is here, Clara. I couldn't stay there, and she... she doesn't belong here."

Clara leaned forward, her elbows on the table. "Ethan, you've been running from that town—and from her—for years. But it doesn't sound like you're running anymore. It sounds like you're stuck."

"I'm not stuck," Ethan shot back, his frustration bubbling to the surface. "I've built something here, something solid. I can't just throw that away."

Clara's expression softened. "I'm not saying you should. But you need to figure out what you want. Because if you keep carrying this weight around, it's going to break you."

Ethan stood abruptly, pacing the small room. "I don't even know what I want, Clara. I thought I did. But seeing her again, being back in that house... it brought everything back."

Clara let the silence stretch for a moment before speaking. "You don't have to figure it all out today. But don't ignore it either. You owe yourself—and her—more than that."

Ethan stopped pacing, his hands on his hips. He looked at Clara, her steady gaze meeting his. "I don't know if I can face it again."

"You already have," Clara said simply. "The question is, what are you going to do about it?"

As the sun set, Ethan sat alone in his office, the stack of projects in front of him forgotten. His mind kept drifting back to Grace, to her smile, her laugh, the way she had looked at him on that last day.

He opened his desk drawer and pulled out a blank sheet of paper. For a long moment, he stared at it, the pen heavy in his hand. Then, slowly, he began to write.

The words came haltingly at first, then faster, spilling onto the page in a torrent. It wasn't a letter this time—it was a confession, an attempt to untangle the mess in his heart.

By the time he finished, the paper was filled, the ink smudged where his hand had trembled. He folded it carefully and slid it into the drawer with the others, a quiet promise to himself that he wasn't ready to make yet.

For now, all he could do was wait.

The days that followed Ethan's return to Gulf City blurred together. He threw himself into work, desperate to distract himself from the memories of Ashville and the lingering ache that Grace had left behind. Yet, no matter how hard he tried to drown himself in the familiar rhythm of his routine, the edges of his thoughts kept drifting back to her.

By midweek, Clara was growing visibly frustrated with his avoidance. She watched him shuffle through meetings and micromanage tasks he usually delegated without a second thought. Finally, she cornered him again—this time at the end of the day when most of the team had gone home.

"Ethan," she said firmly, stepping into his office without knocking. "You've been stomping around here like a storm cloud all week. Either you talk, or I start guessing out loud. And trust me, you don't want me to guess."

Ethan sighed, leaning back in his chair. He rubbed a hand over his face, the exhaustion catching up to him. "Clara, I'm fine."

"You're not," she shot back. "And don't think I didn't notice you spacing out in the middle of the budget meeting. Come on, Ethan. Just tell me what's going on."

Ethan stared at the desk for a long moment before speaking. "I left her letters," he admitted quietly, his voice barely above a whisper.

Clara blinked, her brows furrowing. "Letters?"

"In her mailbox," he continued, as if saying it out loud might make it less real. "I'd written them over the years but never sent them. When I left, I... I couldn't just walk away without leaving something behind."

Clara leaned against the edge of his desk, her arms crossed. "And how do you feel about that?"

"I don't know," Ethan said, his voice tight. "It felt right at the time. But now... I can't stop wondering if I made a mistake. If I should've just told her everything face-to-face."

Clara tilted her head, studying him. "And why didn't you?"

Ethan hesitated, his gaze dropping to the floor. "Because it wouldn't have changed anything. My life is here, Clara. Hers is there. What would've been the point?"

"The point," Clara said gently, "is that you're sitting here torturing yourself over it. Maybe it's not about where your life is, Ethan. Maybe it's about who you want in it."

Ethan shook his head, pushing himself to his feet. "It's not that simple."

"Maybe it is," Clara said, her voice unwavering. "You can build your life around your work, your city, your success. But if you're leaving pieces of yourself behind—like those letters, like Grace—then what are you really building?"

Her words struck a chord, and Ethan felt the weight of them settle on his shoulders. He looked out the window, the lights of the city stretching endlessly before him. It was a life he'd fought for, a life he'd earned. But was it enough?

Clara gave him a moment before speaking again. "Whatever you decide, Ethan, make sure it's something you can live with. Because it sounds like part of you is still standing in Ashville, trying to figure out what you left behind."

Ethan didn't respond, his thoughts too tangled to form words. Clara watched him for a moment longer, then patted his shoulder gently. "You've got time to figure it out. Just don't wait too long."

As the office emptied out and the city settled into its nighttime hum, Ethan found himself alone in his apartment. He sat on the edge of his bed, staring at the packed bag he hadn't fully unpacked since returning.

His phone buzzed on the nightstand, a text from Clara lighting up the screen: *"Don't overthink it. You'll figure it out."*

Ethan sighed, setting the phone down. He opened the drawer of his nightstand and pulled out the shoebox he'd brought back from Ashville—the one that used to hold the letters he'd left behind.

It was empty now, except for one piece of paper tucked into the corner. It was the note Grace had written him the day after his mother's funeral, the one that simply said, *"You're not alone."*

He unfolded it carefully, his fingers brushing over the faded words. For the first time since returning, Ethan allowed himself to hope—just for a moment—that maybe, someday, he could go back.

But for now, all he could do was wait.

Ethan sat at his desk long after the rest of the office had emptied out for the day. The noise of Gulf City hummed faintly in the distance, but it felt far away, muted by the storm inside his head. He had spent the entire day avoiding Clara, dodging her pointed glances and probing questions. He wasn't ready to talk—not yet.

But as the clock ticked toward midnight, he found himself dialing her number. The phone rang twice before Clara answered, her voice warm but slightly surprised.

"Ethan?" she asked. "What's going on? Is everything okay?"

He hesitated, staring out the window at the glowing skyline. "I don't know," he admitted. "Can you come by the office?"

Clara arrived a half hour later, carrying two cups of coffee and a look of quiet concern. She placed one on the desk in front of Ethan and sat across from him.

"Alright," she said, leaning back in the chair. "What's eating you?"

Ethan took a sip of the coffee, grateful for its warmth, and sighed. "I don't know how to do this, Clara. Any of it. Relationships, being close to people... it's like there's this wall, and I can't break through it."

Clara tilted her head, studying him. "You've been through a lot, Ethan. No one comes out of something like that without a few scars."

"It's more than that," he said, his voice raw. "It's like... I'm afraid. Afraid of letting someone in, of getting too close. And I think—I think it's because of him. My father."

Ethan's hands clenched into fists on the desk as he spoke, his voice trembling. "I saw how he treated my mom. How he tore her down piece by piece. And I was too scared to do anything about it. Too small, too weak. And now..."

He paused, struggling to find the words. "Now I'm terrified I'll turn out just like him. That I'll hurt the people I care about the way he did."

Clara leaned forward, her expression softening. "Ethan, you are not your father. You've built a life for yourself that's nothing like his. You've proven time and again that you're capable of love, kindness, and respect. But you've also been running—from him, from Ashville, from everything he represented. And maybe it's time to stop."

Ethan shook his head, his jaw tightening. "You didn't know him, Clara. He wasn't always like that, but something... broke in him. And when it did, it destroyed all of us."

Clara waited, sensing there was more he needed to say.

"It started when he lost his job," Ethan continued, his voice quieter now. "He used to work for a manufacturing company—good pay, stable hours. He was proud of it. Then one day, the company downsized. He came home with a pink slip and a look on his face I'll never forget."

Ethan stared at the coffee in his hands, the memories playing out in his mind like a film. "At first, he tried to find work. Spent hours every day sending out resumes, making calls. But nothing stuck. And after a while, he just... gave up. He started drinking. At first, it was just a beer or two after dinner. But it got worse. And when he drank, he got angry."

Clara nodded slowly, her eyes never leaving his face. "And he took it out on your mom."

Ethan swallowed hard, his throat tightening. "And on me. I tried to stay out of his way, but it didn't matter. He was like a bomb waiting to go off. I promised myself I'd never be like him, that I'd be stronger, better. But now... I don't know. What if it's in me, too?"

Clara reached across the desk, placing a hand on his. "Ethan, your father made choices—bad ones. But you've already made different choices. You've worked hard to build a life, to be better. And yes, you've put up walls, but those walls aren't who you are. They're just a defense. And defenses can be taken down, piece by piece."

Ethan looked at her, his eyes glassy with emotion. "How? How do I even start?"

Clara smiled gently. "By letting yourself believe that you deserve to be loved. By forgiving yourself for the things you couldn't control as a child. And by understanding that your father's pain doesn't have to define yours."

Ethan leaned back in his chair, Clara's words settling over him like a balm. For the first time in a long while, he felt a glimmer of hope—hope that maybe, just maybe, he could find a way to break free of the shadows that had haunted him for so long.

Ethan stared at Clara, his mind a whirlwind of thoughts. He had spent so many years trying to make this life in Gulf City work, trying to convince himself that this was his place, that this was where he was meant to be. But as Clara spoke, something shifted within him, a realization he couldn't ignore.

"This isn't your life, Ethan," Clara said softly, leaning forward. "You've outgrown this place. Gulf City was never meant to be your home. It was a stop—a lesson, a stepping stone. You built what you needed to build here, and you did it well. But now... now it's time to move forward. The threads of fate have always led you exactly where you needed to be, even if you didn't understand it at the time."

Ethan swallowed, his mind reeling.

"You've helped so many people, Ethan," Clara continued, her voice steady, as if she knew exactly what he needed to hear. "You've given this city everything you had. But it's time to go. There's another place waiting for you, another chapter. You can't keep running from it. The people who need you—your family, Grace—those are the people you're meant to be with. You've fulfilled your purpose here."

He looked away, out of the window, but her words settled deep in his chest. There was something freeing about the idea, but also something terrifying. He had fought so hard to build this life. Was he really ready to walk away?

Clara's voice interrupted his thoughts. "You could stay in Ashville. Keep the house. Maybe even set up shop there. You've got the skills, Ethan. The connections. You don't have to stay here just because it's what you've known. If you went back, you could start fresh. You don't have to keep running."

Ethan's gaze drifted back to her. The idea of returning to Ashville—of staying there, living there—was both familiar and foreign. That town had always felt like a cage to him, a place that trapped him in the past. But now? Now it was different. Now, it held a key to his future.

He rubbed the back of his neck, the weight of the decision pressing down on him. "I've built so much here. A life I can be proud of. I didn't want to leave it behind... I didn't want to leave all this. But it was never meant to be here. Gulf City wasn't meant to be my home."

Clara watched him carefully, her eyes softening with understanding. "No. Gulf City was never your home. You've learned the lessons, Ethan. You've grown into the man you were always meant to become. But you're not meant to stay here. You have more to do. You have people to love, people to help, people who need you."

The silence in the room grew heavy as Ethan absorbed her words. It was true. Gulf City had been a chapter—an important one, yes, but still only a chapter. He had come here, rebuilt himself, and grown in ways he never thought possible. But the pull of Ashville, the people waiting for him, the unfinished business... it was calling him back.

Clara's voice broke through his thoughts again, more gentle this time. "You've done great things here, Ethan. But sometimes... sometimes the best thing we can do for ourselves is to let go. Let go of what we think we need, and step into what we were always meant to have."

Ethan felt his heart begin to settle, a calm taking over him, as if he were beginning to understand the pieces of the puzzle falling into place.

"You're right," he said, his voice barely above a whisper. "I've been holding on to this life, but it's not mine. It's not meant for me. I've learned everything I needed to here, but it's time to go. Time to go back home."

Clara smiled, her expression a mixture of pride and quiet sadness. "Then go, Ethan. Go where you're needed. The people here—your employees, your friends—they won't resent you. They won't forget you. You've done more than enough for Gulf City. But the people who really matter... they're waiting for you."

Ethan sat back in his chair, his fingers tapping absentmindedly on the desk. He wasn't sure how much time had passed, but the weight of Clara's words had planted something deep within him. He could feel the stirrings of something new—something powerful. A future that had always been just beyond his reach was now unfolding before him, slowly, but steadily.

He thought about Grace, about the way she had stood by him without question, without hesitation. She had always been there—his anchor, his touchstone. The time they had spent together in Ashville had brought them closer than he ever could have imagined.

He knew what he had to do. There was no more running, no more hiding. Ashville was where he needed to be. With Grace. With the people who had never given up on him, even when he had given up on himself.

As the final words echoed in his mind, Ethan stood, a sense of purpose flooding his chest. He was done with uncertainty. He was done with fear. The choice was clear.

It was time to go home.

Chapter Seven

Ethan stood at the door of his Gulf City office, the weight of everything on his shoulders. The days since his decision to leave had passed in a blur—tasks to finish, conversations to have, paperwork to sign, and a future that still felt uncertain no matter how certain he was about it. It had taken him years to build what he had here, but only days to make the decision to leave it all behind. There was a sadness in him, but there was something else too—relief.

Today was the last day.

The place that had become a second home, a place where he had made a name for himself, was going to be left behind. He had told Clara everything, every feeling that had been bottled up for so long, and now it was time to wrap up his responsibilities. The final bit of paperwork, the last of the projects—he checked them all off one by one, and each task felt like a stone lifting from his chest.

Clara had been understanding, her steady presence reassuring, but the goodbyes were still heavy. There was no avoiding it. She would be taking over, running the business. She was ready. Ethan had seen that, but he couldn't deny that leaving was difficult. His life here had been significant, and he had made his mark. Gulf City had given him so much, but it was never truly his home.

He walked through the office one last time, the empty halls echoing his every step. The conference room, where he'd made deals and decisions, the breakroom where he had shared countless conversations with his employees. All of it was about to be someone else's. All of it would be Clara's now.

His fingers traced the edge of his desk, the leather of the chair where he had sat countless hours. He had learned a lot here—about business, about people, about himself. But none of that was enough to keep him. None of it could fill the void he had tried so desperately to ignore for so long.

The next two days were a blur of goodbyes. Ethan didn't try to make it dramatic. He didn't want to make a spectacle of it. He just made sure everything was in order, that the people who depended on him were taken care of, and that Clara had what she needed to continue the work he had started.

He made a point to visit Joe, who had always greeted him with a smile, no matter how bad the day had been. He walked into the food truck with a heavy heart, but he knew it was the right thing to do.

"You leaving, huh?" Joe asked, a wry grin on his face. "I guess you finally figured it out."

Ethan nodded. "Yeah, I did."

Joe slapped him on the back. "Well, don't be a stranger. You did good here. We all appreciate you."

Ethan gave a tight smile, the lump in his throat threatening to make him lose his composure. "I'll never forget you, Joe. You were the first person who didn't look at me like I was just some guy off the street. You fed me when I had nothing."

Joe waved it off. "We all gotta look out for each other, right? Take care of yourself, Ethan. You earned it."

Then there was Maria, the woman who had always been so quiet but so steady in her own way. She had learned from him and in turn, he had learned from her. Her quiet wisdom had always grounded him.

"I never thought I'd see the day," Maria said softly when he said goodbye. "You've come a long way, Ethan. I'm proud of you, mijo."

Ethan's chest tightened. "I'm proud of you, too. You've got a good heart, Maria. Keep it that way."

By the time he finished up everything in Gulf City, Ethan was exhausted. It wasn't physical fatigue—it was the emotional toll of closing a chapter of his life that he had fought so hard to make. But it was time to move on. It was time to go home. To Ashville. To Grace.

Ethan's car rumbled to a stop in front of Grace's house, the engine's hum fading into the quiet hum of the town. He sat there for a long moment, his hands gripping the steering wheel, his chest tight with nerves. This wasn't like walking into the lawyer's office or stepping into his childhood home. This was different—this was personal.

The house stood quietly, a testament to Grace's life and resilience. It was small but well-kept, with flower beds lining the porch and wind chimes swaying gently in the breeze. It suited her perfectly—warm, inviting, with a touch of the past mingling with the present. For a moment, he just stared, as if trying to summon the courage to step out of the car.

When he finally moved, it was with the hesitancy of a man about to face his past head-on. His shoes crunched against the gravel as he walked up the path to her door. Each step felt heavier than the last, his heart thudding in his chest. This wasn't just about Grace. It was about everything he'd left behind—the promises he didn't keep, the person he tried to forget.

He raised a hand to knock, then hesitated. What if she wasn't home? What if she didn't want to see him? What if... No. He shook his head, steeling himself. This was why he came back. He needed to say everything he hadn't said before, to give them both the closure—or the beginning—they deserved.

The door opened before he could knock.

Grace stood there, framed by the soft glow of the afternoon sun. She looked the same and yet different, time having added subtle changes—a few lines near her eyes, a certain depth to her expression—but her presence was as grounding as ever. Her dark hair was pulled back loosely, and she wore a simple sweater that made her look effortlessly beautiful.

For a moment, they just stared at each other, the weight of years pressing down on the space between them.

"Ethan," she said softly, her voice carrying a mix of surprise and something unreadable.

"Grace," he managed, his voice barely above a whisper. His throat felt dry, and he swallowed hard. "I… I had to come."

She didn't move for a moment, as if debating whether to invite him in or leave him standing there. Then, with a slight nod, she stepped aside, holding the door open. "Come in."

The house smelled of cinnamon and something faintly floral, a scent that instantly reminded him of her. He stepped inside, his hands in his pockets, feeling strangely out of place despite her welcoming presence. The living room was cozy, filled with personal touches—books stacked on a side table, a throw blanket draped over the arm of a chair, photographs of her family and friends on the walls.

He stood awkwardly for a moment until she motioned toward the couch. "Sit down."

He did, his heart still pounding. Grace sat across from him in an armchair, her hands folded in her lap. For a moment, the silence was deafening, each of them waiting for the other to speak.

Finally, Ethan broke it. "I didn't know where else to go."

Grace tilted her head, studying him. "You've always known where to go, Ethan. You just didn't want to come here."

Her words weren't harsh, but they struck a chord deep within him. He looked down at his hands, clasped tightly together. "I'm sorry," he said quietly. "For leaving. For everything."

She didn't respond immediately, and the silence stretched again. When she finally spoke, her voice was calm but tinged with emotion. "Why now? Why come back now?"

He looked up, meeting her gaze. "Because I couldn't stay away anymore. I thought I could build a life somewhere else, that I could forget... everything. But I was wrong. Everywhere I went, I carried Ashville with me. I carried you with me."

Her breath hitched slightly, and she looked away, blinking rapidly. "You left, I thought things were going to be different," she said, her voice barely above a whisper. "You didn't even give me a chance to understand."

"I know," he admitted, his voice raw. "I thought it would be easier that way. For both of us. But it wasn't. I've spent every day since wondering what might have been, what I could have done differently."

Grace looked back at him, her eyes glistening with unshed tears. "You don't get to just walk back in and fix everything, Ethan."

"I'm not trying to fix everything," he said earnestly. "I know I can't. But I need you to know... I need you to know that leaving was the hardest thing I've ever done. And it wasn't because I didn't care. It was because I cared too much."

Her expression softened slightly, but she didn't speak. The weight of his words hung in the air, filling the room with a mix of pain and hope.

"I don't know what I'm expecting," he continued, his voice quieter now. "I don't even know if there's anything left to fix. But I couldn't leave again without telling you the truth."

Grace leaned back in her chair, exhaling slowly. "And what is the truth, Ethan?"

He leaned forward, resting his elbows on his knees, his eyes locked on hers. "The truth is, I've never stopped thinking about you. About us. About everything we could have been."

Her lips parted slightly, as if she wanted to respond but didn't know how. The vulnerability in her eyes mirrored his own, and for a moment, it felt like they were back in time, before everything went wrong.

Grace's gaze softened, but her posture remained guarded. She tucked a strand of hair behind her ear, a telltale sign that she was nervous. "I got the letters," she said quietly, breaking the silence between them.

Ethan froze, his breath catching in his throat. "You... you read them?"

She nodded, her lips pressing into a thin line. "Every single one." Her voice wavered, as though each word carried its own weight. "I wasn't sure what to think at first. I mean, who does that? Writing letters and never sending them?"

"I thought it was better that way," Ethan admitted, his voice barely above a whisper. He looked down, unable to meet her eyes. "I didn't think you'd ever want to hear from me. After the way I left..." He trailed off, the guilt curling around his words like smoke.

Grace's expression was unreadable as she leaned forward slightly. "Those letters... they weren't just words, Ethan. They were pieces of you. And every time I read one, I felt like I was being pulled back into something I thought I'd let go of."

Ethan swallowed hard, his heart thudding painfully in his chest. "I didn't mean to hurt you all over again," he said, his voice raw. "I just... I couldn't stop writing. It was the only way I knew how to keep you close, even if you didn't know."

Grace looked away, her fingers fidgeting with the hem of her sweater. "Some of them made me laugh," she admitted after a pause. "You always had a way with words, even when you were just rambling about nothing. But some of them..." She hesitated, her voice trembling slightly. "Some of them broke me."

Ethan's chest tightened, the weight of her words hitting him like a freight train. "I'm sorry," he said, his voice thick with emotion. "I never wanted that."

Grace shook her head, a tear slipping down her cheek. She quickly wiped it away, as though trying to maintain some semblance of composure. "You don't get it, Ethan. Those letters were all I had of you. And for years, I convinced myself that I was better off without you. That I was fine. But then you showed up again, and everything... everything came rushing back."

Ethan stood abruptly, pacing the small living room as he ran a hand through his hair. "I don't know how to make this right," he admitted, his voice cracking. "I've been running my whole life, Grace. From this town, from my past... from you. And now, standing here, I realize I can't run anymore. Not from you."

Grace looked up at him, her eyes shimmering with unshed tears. "Then don't," she said simply, her voice barely above a whisper. "Don't run this time, Ethan."

Her words hung in the air, heavy with meaning. Ethan stopped pacing, his eyes locking onto hers. For a moment, the room felt too small to contain everything between them—the hope, the fear, the unspoken possibilities.

"I'm scared," he admitted, his voice trembling. "I'm scared that I'll screw this up again. That I'll hurt you."

Grace stood then, crossing the small distance between them. She placed a hand on his arm, grounding him. "You're not your father, Ethan," she said firmly, her voice steady despite the tears in her eyes. "You don't have to be him. And you don't have to run anymore. But you have to decide. You can't keep one foot in the past and one in the future. You have to choose."

Ethan looked down at her, his heart aching with the weight of her words. "I don't know how to choose," he admitted. "I don't even know if I'm strong enough."

Grace's gaze didn't waver. "You've always been strong enough. You just have to believe it."

For a long moment, they stood there in silence, the unspoken emotions between them almost palpable. Finally, Ethan exhaled, his shoulders sagging slightly. "I want to believe it," he said softly. "I want to believe that I can be the person you deserve."

Grace smiled faintly, her hand still resting on his arm. "Then start by staying. Start by letting yourself be here, with me."

Ethan felt something shift inside him, a flicker of hope breaking through the darkness. He wasn't sure where this path would lead, but for the first time in years, he felt like he wasn't walking it alone.

Ethan took a shaky breath, his eyes fixed on Grace as if anchoring himself to her. "You make it sound so easy," he said, his voice tinged with vulnerability. "But it's not. Staying means facing everything I've buried for so long. It means… risking everything."

Grace's hand lingered on his arm, her touch a quiet reassurance. "It's not easy, Ethan," she admitted. "Nothing worth having ever is. But you've already taken the hardest step—coming back. The rest? That's just figuring out where you want to be."

He hesitated, his gaze falling to the floor. "I thought I'd figured it out," he murmured. "The life I built in Gulf City... it felt safe. Controlled. But being here, with you... it's like everything I thought I knew is unraveling."

Grace tilted her head, studying him. "Maybe it's not unraveling," she suggested gently. "Maybe it's just shifting, making room for something better."

Ethan let her words sink in, the possibility both terrifying and exhilarating. "When I left, I told myself it was for the best. That I was protecting you from... well, from me. But now, I wonder if I was just protecting myself. I didn't want to face how much it hurt to lose you."

Grace stepped closer, her voice soft but firm. "And what about now? Are you still trying to protect yourself? Or are you ready to face it?"

The question hung in the air, and Ethan felt the weight of it pressing down on him. He thought about the letters he'd written, each one a desperate attempt to keep her close even when he couldn't be. He thought about the house, the echoes of his past, and the scars he'd carried for so long.

Finally, he looked up, meeting her gaze. "I don't want to lose you again," he admitted, his voice breaking. "But I don't know how to be the person you need me to be."

Grace's expression softened, and she reached up to touch his cheek, her fingers light against his skin. "You don't have to be perfect, Ethan," she said. "You just have to be honest. With me. With yourself."

Her touch was his undoing. He closed his eyes, leaning into her hand as a tear slipped down his cheek. "I'm scared, Grace," he whispered. "But I don't want to run anymore."

She smiled faintly, her own eyes glistening. "Then don't. Stay."

The simplicity of her words broke something open inside him. For so long, he'd been running—away from his past, away from his pain, away from her. But now, standing here with Grace, he felt a glimmer of something he hadn't allowed himself to feel in years: hope.

"I don't know what staying looks like," he said after a moment. "I don't even know where to start."

Grace lowered her hand but didn't step back, her presence grounding him. "We start where we are," she said. "One step at a time. Together."

Ethan nodded slowly, the weight of his fear beginning to lift. For the first time in a long time, he allowed himself to imagine a future—one where he wasn't running, where he wasn't alone.

"I'd like that," he said softly, his voice steady despite the emotions swirling inside him. "I'd like to try."

Grace smiled, the kind of smile that made everything else fade away. "Then we try," she said simply.

For the rest of the evening, they sat together, talking about everything and nothing. The heaviness of their earlier conversation lingered, but it was balanced by a newfound lightness, a tentative hope. They didn't have all the answers, but for the first time, it felt like they were asking the right questions—together.

Chapter Eight

The morning light filtered through the thin curtains of the motel room Ethan had rented, bathing the small space in a soft, golden glow. He stared at the ceiling, his mind drifting over the conversation with Grace from the night before. It had left him raw, but for the first time in years, he didn't feel untethered.

The bundle of emotions from their talk still pressed heavily on him: the hope, the fear, and the fragile sense of possibility. But this morning felt different. There was a calmness to it, as if the town itself had shifted, making room for him in its rhythm. Ashville wasn't home yet—but maybe, just maybe, it could be.

Ethan sat up slowly, swinging his legs over the side of the bed. The cool wooden floor beneath his feet grounded him, a reminder that today marked a beginning. No more running, no more hiding. It was time to see what staying looked like.

The first thing he did was drive to the house. The "For Sale" sign was still planted firmly in the yard, but as Ethan parked the car, the idea of selling felt less certain. He stepped out and took a deep breath, the crisp morning air filling his lungs. The house had loomed large in his nightmares, a place of so much pain, but standing here now, he saw something else: potential.

The repairs he and Grace had made had softened its edges, transformed it into something that could be livable. Maybe even a home.

"Morning," came a voice, pulling him from his thoughts. He turned to find Grace standing on the sidewalk, holding two cups of coffee. She smiled, holding one out to him.

"Morning," he replied, taking the cup with a nod of thanks. "You're up early."

She shrugged, taking a sip of her own drink. "Couldn't sleep. Thought I'd check on you. Figured you'd be here."

Ethan smirked faintly, shaking his head. "You know me too well."

"Someone has to," she teased lightly before her expression softened. "How're you feeling?"

He took a slow sip of coffee, considering her question. "Like I'm starting over," he admitted. "It's… unsettling. But not bad."

Grace studied him for a moment before nodding. "Starting over isn't easy," she said. "But it's worth it."

Ethan looked at her, his chest tightening with something unspoken. For so long, he'd kept himself at arm's length, even from her. But now, he wasn't sure he could anymore. "Thanks," he said quietly, his voice thick with meaning.

Grace smiled, her eyes warm. "You don't have to thank me, Ethan. I'm just glad you're here."

The day unfolded slowly, the way mornings in small towns often did. Ethan spent time walking through the house, taking in the work they'd done and making mental notes of what still needed to be handled. Grace stayed with him, helping him measure a window frame for new curtains and sharing stories about the town's recent history.

By midday, they stood in the backyard, surveying the overgrown garden. Grace pointed out a corner where his mother used to plant flowers when he was a child, reminiscing about the blooms that once brightened the space. Ethan found himself imagining what it would look like restored—a vibrant burst of color against the house's pale siding.

"This place doesn't have to be a prison, you know," Grace said after a moment, her voice gentle. "It could be something good."

Ethan glanced at her, the weight of her words sinking in. "Maybe," he said, his tone uncertain but not dismissive. "It's just hard to see it that way."

Grace tilted her head, giving him a thoughtful look. "You don't have to see it all at once. Sometimes it's enough to take the first step."

Her words stayed with him as the day wore on, echoing in his mind as he began to make a mental list of what staying in Ashville might look like—not just for the house, but for him.

As the sun began to set, Ethan realized he felt something he hadn't in years: a cautious, fragile sense of belonging.

Ethan stood on the front porch, staring at the "For Sale" sign that had been his silent companion since his return. The bold letters had once felt like a promise, a guarantee that he could shed the weight of this house and all it represented. Now, it felt like a wall between who he was and who he wanted to become.

His hand tightened around the phone as he finished the call to the realtor. The conversation had been brief, but its significance was profound. The house was officially off the market.

He slipped the phone into his pocket and looked back at the door. Grace was inside, humming softly to herself as she sorted through the boxes in the living room. For the first time, Ethan allowed himself to think of this house not as a monument to his father's rage but as a blank slate—a place where he could build something better.

Inside, Grace was crouched by a stack of boxes, her hands covered in dust. She looked up as he walked in, brushing a stray strand of hair from her face. "You've been quiet," she said, studying him. "What's on your mind?"

Ethan leaned against the doorframe, his arms crossed. "I took the house off the market."

Grace blinked, surprised. "You did?"

He nodded, his gaze fixed on the worn floorboards. "Yeah. I think... I think I'm staying."

A slow smile spread across her face, but she tempered it, searching his expression for hesitation. "Are you sure? This isn't something you have to rush into."

"I'm sure," he said firmly. "Selling it wouldn't change anything. It wouldn't erase the past, and it wouldn't give me what I've been looking for. Maybe this house doesn't have to be a reminder of what happened. Maybe it can be... something else."

Grace stood, wiping her hands on her jeans. "Something good."

Ethan's lips twitched into a small smile. "Something good."

The next few days were a whirlwind of activity. Grace helped Ethan put the finishing touches on the house, from repainting the last few scuffed walls to replacing the worn-out curtains. They worked side by side, the rhythm of their shared tasks weaving a quiet intimacy between them.

In the attic, they found an old wooden chest tucked into the corner. Ethan pried it open, revealing a collection of yellowed letters and faded photographs. Among them was a picture of his parents on their wedding day, their smiles unrecognizable from the faces he remembered.

Grace knelt beside him, looking at the photo. "They look happy," she said softly.

"They were, once," Ethan murmured, running his thumb over the edge of the picture. "Before everything fell apart."

Grace placed a hand on his arm. "You're not him, Ethan. You don't have to carry his mistakes."

He nodded, swallowing the lump in his throat. "I know. But it's hard not to feel like I'm tied to it."

"You're not," she said firmly. "You're here now, and you're making your own choices. That's what matters."

In the backyard, they planted a small flower bed in the corner Grace had pointed out earlier. It wasn't much—just a few daisies and marigolds—but it felt like a declaration. The yard, like the house, was slowly becoming his.

As they finished, Grace leaned against the fence, watching the sunset cast a golden glow over the town. "It's strange," she said after a moment. "I always thought you'd leave again. That you wouldn't be able to stay."

"I thought so too," Ethan admitted, standing beside her. "But I'm tired of running."

Grace turned to him, her gaze steady. "So, what now?"

He looked at her, the answer coming to him as easily as breathing. "Now, I make this my home."

Her lips curved into a soft smile. "Sounds like a good plan."

For the first time in years, Ethan felt a sense of peace settle over him. The house was no longer a place of fear. It was his—his to rebuild, his to heal in, his to share.

Ethan stood on the main street of Ashville, staring at the empty storefront that would soon house his new furniture repair shop. The building was unassuming—a modest brick structure with wide windows that overlooked the bustling town square. It wasn't much, but it was enough. It was a beginning.

Grace stepped up beside him, her hands in her jacket pockets, and tilted her head as she took in the sight. "It's got potential," she said with a grin.

"Potential?" Ethan raised an eyebrow, smirking. "That's one way to put it."

She nudged him playfully. "Don't knock it. You're going to make it into something amazing. I know you will."

Ethan glanced at her, warmth spreading through him at her confidence. He still wasn't used to having someone believe in him this much. "You're really that sure of me, huh?"

Grace turned to him, her expression soft but unwavering. "Ethan, I've always believed in you. Even when you didn't."

Her words stayed with him as they stepped inside the building. The interior was dusty and cluttered with remnants of its former life—a hardware store that had closed years ago. Ethan walked through the space, imagining rows of polished tables and chairs, the scent of freshly cut wood filling the air.

"This could work," he murmured to himself, a spark of determination igniting in his chest.

Over the following weeks, Ethan threw himself into transforming the space. Grace was there every step of the way, from painting the walls to sanding down reclaimed wood for shelves. Together, they built workbenches and repaired old tools, turning the empty shell of a building into something that reflected Ethan's vision.

The town watched with curiosity. At first, there were whispers—questions about whether Ethan Blackwell could really leave behind the shadow of his father. But as the shop took shape, those whispers turned into cautious support. People stopped by to offer advice, lend tools, or simply chat with Ethan and Grace about their progress.

One afternoon, as Ethan worked on a display counter near the storefront window, an older man stepped inside. He wore overalls and carried a small wooden stool with a broken leg.

"You're the Blackwell boy, aren't you?" the man asked, his voice gruff but not unkind.

Ethan straightened, wiping his hands on his jeans. "Yes, sir. That's me."

The man set the stool on the counter. "Heard you were opening up a furniture repair shop. Thought I'd bring this by, see if you're as good as they say."

Ethan hesitated, the weight of the man's expectations pressing on him. Then he caught Grace's encouraging smile from where she was organizing tools in the back. He picked up the stool, examining the damage. "I'll take care of it," he said confidently. "Come back in a couple of days, and it'll be good as new."

The man nodded, tipping his hat before leaving. Ethan exhaled, glancing at Grace. "Think I passed the first test?"

She chuckled, walking over to him. "You're doing more than that, Ethan. They're starting to see you for who you really are."

As the weeks turned into months, the shop became a cornerstone of the community. Ethan repaired tables and chairs, restored family heirlooms, and even crafted new pieces for the townspeople. Each project felt like a step toward redemption—a way to prove to himself and to Ashville that he was more than his father's son.

Grace became his unofficial partner, handling the business side of things and greeting customers with her warm smile. They fell into an easy rhythm, their bond growing stronger with each passing day.

One evening, after locking up the shop, Ethan and Grace sat on the front steps, watching the sun set over the town square.

"You've done it," Grace said, breaking the comfortable silence. "You've made this place your own."

Ethan leaned back, resting his elbows on the step behind him. "We've done it," he corrected. "I couldn't have done any of this without you."

She smiled, but there was a flicker of something in her eyes—something Ethan couldn't quite place. "You've always had it in you, Ethan. You just needed to see it for yourself."

He reached over, covering her hand with his. "I see it now. And I'm not going anywhere."

Grace looked at him, her expression softening. "Good. Because Ashville needs you. And... so do I."

The weight of her words settled over him, filling the spaces in his heart he hadn't realized were still empty. For the first time in his life, Ethan felt like he was exactly where he was meant to be.

Ethan leaned against the counter of his newly established shop, carefully inspecting the intricate carving on a restored dining table. The scent of sawdust and varnish filled the air, a comforting reminder of how far he'd come. Business had been steady since the shop opened, but he still hadn't landed a major project—something that could put him on the map and solidify his place in Ashville.

As if summoned by the thought, the bell above the door jingled. Ethan looked up to see a sharply dressed man with a clipboard in hand stepping inside. The man's gaze swept over the workshop before settling on Ethan.

"Ethan Blackwell?" the man asked.

"That's me," Ethan replied, setting the carving tool down.

The man extended a hand. "Robert Hale. I represent Southern Ridge Furniture, the manufacturer just outside of town. We're in a bit of a situation, and your name came highly recommended."

Ethan shook his hand, curiosity piqued. "What kind of situation?"

Robert glanced around the shop again, his expression thoughtful. "We've been commissioned to supply a series of handcrafted tables and chairs for an art gallery in Gulf City. Problem is, it's a custom order, and our in-house team doesn't have the expertise to pull it off. Word around town is that you're the man to see for this kind of work."

Ethan's chest tightened at the mention of Gulf City. His mind immediately flashed to Clara and the gallery where he'd first honed his craft. He hadn't expected to hear that name so soon.

"I might be able to help," Ethan said carefully. "What's the timeline?"

Robert grimaced. "That's the catch. The deadline is tight—six weeks. But it's a lucrative deal, and if you pull it off, it could mean big things for your shop."

Ethan looked at the sketches Robert handed him. The designs were intricate but manageable, each piece blending artistic flair with functionality. He could see why the manufacturer needed help; this wasn't standard mass production.

"I'll do it," Ethan said after a moment's hesitation.

Robert smiled, relief evident on his face. "You'll have full creative control over the designs, and we'll provide any additional materials or manpower you need."

The next day, Grace joined Ethan at the shop as he reviewed the project details. She sat across from him at the workbench, flipping through the design sketches.

"This is a big deal," she said, her voice tinged with excitement.

"Yeah," Ethan replied, though his tone was more measured. "It's also a lot of pressure. If I mess this up—"

"You won't," Grace interrupted firmly. She reached across the table, her hand brushing his. "You're more than capable, Ethan. And Gulf City already knows that. This is your chance to show Ashville what you're made of."

Her confidence in him was unwavering, and it gave Ethan the boost he needed. Over the next few days, he poured himself into the project. Grace became his sounding board, helping him refine ideas and manage the growing workload.

As the pieces began to take shape, Ethan couldn't help but reflect on his time in Gulf City. The gallery there had been a turning point in his life, a place where he had discovered his talent and built his confidence. Now, years later, the opportunity to create for that same gallery felt like coming full circle.

One evening, as he and Grace sanded down a set of chair legs, Ethan paused. "It's strange, isn't it? How everything's connected. Gulf City, Clara, this gallery... it's like the threads of fate are weaving something bigger than I can see."

Grace looked up, her eyes soft. "Maybe they are. But don't forget, you're the one weaving those threads, Ethan. This is your story, and you're the one making it happen."

Her words stayed with him as the project progressed.

Six weeks later, the final pieces were loaded onto a truck bound for Gulf City. The tables and chairs gleamed under the shop's overhead lights, each one a testament to Ethan's skill and determination.

As the truck pulled away, Ethan stood with Grace outside the shop, watching until it disappeared down the road.

"You did it," Grace said, her voice filled with pride.

Ethan nodded, a sense of accomplishment settling over him. "We did it."

Grace smiled, and for a moment, they stood in silence, the future stretching out before them like an unwritten chapter.

The shop felt strangely quiet after the truck departed, as though it, too, had exhaled after weeks of relentless energy. Ethan and Grace lingered by the door, neither in a hurry to leave.

"That was a big moment, wasn't it?" Grace asked, her hands tucked into her jacket pockets.

Ethan leaned against the frame of the door, his gaze fixed on the fading streaks of the truck's taillights. "It feels like it. But it also feels... unfinished. Like there's more to do."

Grace turned to face him, a gentle smile tugging at her lips. "There always will be, Ethan. But that doesn't mean you can't celebrate what you've accomplished."

Ethan's smile was faint, but it was there. "I guess I just don't know how to slow down. Gulf City was all about the hustle—one project after another. But here... here, it's different. It's not just about the work."

"It's about belonging," Grace finished softly.

Ethan glanced at her, surprised by how effortlessly she could put his thoughts into words. "Yeah. It is."

Later that evening, Ethan sat on the front steps of his shop, the cool Ashville air wrapping around him. Grace had gone home, insisting that he take the night to rest and recharge. But rest was elusive, his thoughts swirling like autumn leaves in the breeze.

He thought about the man he'd been in Gulf City—ambitious, determined, but always looking for something he couldn't quite name. And now, standing on the threshold of a new life in Ashville, he wondered if he'd finally found it.

The faint sound of footsteps pulled him from his thoughts. He looked up to see Clara approaching, her ever-present warmth in her expression.

"You didn't think I'd miss your big moment, did you?" she said, holding up a small box wrapped in brown paper.

"Clara," Ethan said, rising to greet her. "What are you doing here?"

"Business brought me to the area, but I figured I'd make time for an old friend," she said, handing him the box. "Go on, open it."

Ethan carefully unwrapped the paper, revealing a small wooden plaque. *Blackwell & Co. Furniture Restoration: Ashville, WI.*

"It's beautiful," he said, his voice thick with emotion.

Clara smiled. "It's official now. You're not just passing through anymore, Ethan. This place is your home."

Ethan's grip tightened on the plaque as he looked at her. "I couldn't have done any of this without you. You know that, right?"

Clara waved a hand dismissively. "Oh, please. You had it in you all along. I just gave you the tools to see it."

The next day, Ethan and Grace walked the length of Main Street, her hand lightly brushing his as they strolled.

"You're quiet today," she said, glancing at him.

"I'm just thinking about what's next," he admitted. "The shop is up and running, but there's still so much I want to do."

Grace tilted her head. "Like what?"

"Like making this town my home. For real this time," he said, his voice steady.

Grace's smile was soft, her eyes glinting with unspoken emotion. "I think you're already on your way."

Ethan stood at the base of the old oak tree, craning his neck to look up at the rickety structure nestled in its branches. The treehouse was still standing, though barely. Time and neglect had taken their toll—planks were missing, the roof sagged, and vines tangled around the supports like nature's attempt to reclaim it.

"I can't believe it's still here," Grace said, standing beside him. She shaded her eyes with her hand, peering up at the battered remains. "I haven't thought about this place in years."

Ethan chuckled softly. "Neither have I. Back then, it felt indestructible. Like it was its own little world, safe from everything else."

Grace turned to him, a playful glint in her eyes. "Your kingdom, wasn't it? You were the king, self-proclaimed and all."

Ethan smirked. "Well, someone had to keep the peace. But it's nothing without its queen."

The words slipped out before he could stop them, and for a moment, they both froze. Grace's gaze lingered on him, her expression softening into something he couldn't quite name.

"Let's clear it out," she said suddenly, breaking the tension.

Ethan blinked. "What?"

"The treehouse," Grace said, already stepping toward the base of the trunk. "Let's clear it out. Bring it back to life."

"You're serious?"

"Dead serious." She shot him a grin over her shoulder. "Unless, of course, the mighty king is afraid of a little hard work."

Ethan laughed, shaking his head. "All right, then. Let's do it."

The next few hours were a flurry of activity. Armed with gloves, pruning shears, and sheer determination, they hacked away at the vines that clung to the supports. Dead branches and leaves were tossed into a growing pile nearby, and Ethan couldn't help but marvel at how easily they fell into their old rhythm.

"This thing's a mess," Ethan muttered as he pried loose a stubborn vine.

Grace laughed. "Well, it's been abandoned for, what, two decades? Give it some credit for holding on this long."

Ethan paused, his gaze drifting to the worn planks of the treehouse. "I guess it's kind of like us, huh? Still standing after all this time, even if it's a little worse for wear."

Grace stilled, her expression unreadable. "Yeah," she said softly. "I guess it is."

They worked in companionable silence for a while, the air filled with the rustle of leaves and the occasional creak of wood. As they cleared away the debris, memories began to surface—half-forgotten adventures and whispered secrets from their childhood.

"Remember the time we tried to build a pulley system up there?" Grace asked, gesturing toward the platform.

Ethan grinned. "How could I forget? It collapsed the second I tested it. You laughed so hard, I thought you'd fall out of the tree."

"I wasn't laughing at you!" Grace protested, though her smile betrayed her. "I was laughing because you were fine and still so proud of it."

"Well, it was a good idea in theory," Ethan said, chuckling.

By late afternoon, the treehouse was free of vines and debris, its bones exposed to the world once more. It wasn't much to look at, but to Ethan, it felt like a victory.

"We'll need new planks for the floor," Grace said, her hands on her hips as she surveyed their work. "And probably new supports for the roof. Oh, and paint. Lots of paint."

Ethan glanced at her, a small smile tugging at his lips. "You're really into this, aren't you?"

Grace shrugged, her cheeks faintly pink. "Well, it was your kingdom. It only seems right to bring it back to life."

"Our kingdom," Ethan corrected.

She looked at him, her smile softening. "Our kingdom, then."

Ethan's chest tightened, an ache he couldn't quite name settling in his heart. For the first time in years, the future didn't feel like a distant, uncertain thing. It felt tangible, like something he could hold onto.

"And when it's done," he said, his voice steady, "you'll be the queen. Officially."

Grace laughed, a sound that warmed him to his core. "Well, it's about time."

Ethan wiped the sweat from his brow as the late afternoon sun filtered through the tree's branches. The two of them had made significant progress. The rotted planks were gone, and the new wood they had brought earlier that day leaned neatly against the base of the tree. Grace had taken it upon herself to sketch a rough plan for the treehouse's restoration on a notepad, crouched in the shade with a pencil tucked behind her ear.

"It's not a kingdom without a throne," Grace said, squinting down at her drawing.

Ethan smirked as he set another discarded plank onto the pile. "A throne, huh? Should I carve it out of the finest wood in Ashville?"

"Absolutely," Grace replied, grinning up at him. "Anything less would be unacceptable."

Ethan chuckled, leaning against the tree trunk. "You always did have a way of turning my ideas into something better."

Grace's smile softened, her pencil stalling over the paper. "I don't know about that. You've always been the dreamer, Ethan. I just... added a little flair."

He watched her for a moment, the light catching in her hair as she focused on the sketch. It was in these quiet moments, working side by side, that the walls between them seemed to crumble.

Later that evening, as the last rays of sunlight painted the sky in hues of gold and pink, they sat on the edge of the treehouse's platform. The structure was far from complete, but the floor was sturdy enough to hold them. Ethan leaned back on his hands, gazing out at the yard below, while Grace hugged her knees to her chest.

"This feels... surreal," Grace murmured, breaking the comfortable silence. "Sitting here again, like we're kids and nothing ever changed."

Ethan nodded. "Yeah. It's almost like time hasn't passed at all."

Grace glanced at him, her expression contemplative. "Do you ever wonder what would've happened if you'd stayed? If you'd never left Ashville?"

He hesitated, her question hanging in the air between them. "All the time," he admitted. "But back then... staying didn't feel like an option. I had to get away from here, from him. It was the only way I thought I could survive."

Grace nodded slowly, understanding etched across her face. "I get that. But I also know it wasn't just about him. You were afraid of becoming him, weren't you?"

Ethan stiffened, her words cutting through him like a blade. "Yeah," he said after a moment, his voice barely above a whisper. "I watched what he did to my mom, how he tore her down piece by piece. I couldn't let myself become that."

Grace reached out, her hand brushing against his. "You're not him, Ethan. You never were."

Her words struck something deep inside him, a crack forming in the armor he had built over the years. "Sometimes it feels like I've spent my whole life running," he said. "From this place, from the past, from myself. But maybe..." He paused, swallowing hard. "Maybe it's time I stopped."

Grace's fingers tightened around his. "You've already started, Ethan. You're here, aren't you?"

The next day, they resumed their work on the treehouse, the atmosphere between them lighter, as if the previous night's conversation had lifted a weight from both their shoulders.

Grace handed Ethan a hammer, her brow furrowed in concentration. "Okay, so this plank goes... here, right?"

Ethan nodded, crouching beside her to guide the wood into place. "You've got a good eye for this."

"Don't sound so surprised," she teased, nudging him with her elbow. "I did help build the original, remember?"

He grinned, shaking his head. "You mean you supervised while mom and I did all the work."

"Hey, supervision is an important skill!" she shot back, laughing.

Their laughter echoed through the yard, blending with the rhythmic sound of hammering and the occasional creak of the treehouse as it took shape. With each nail driven into the wood, Ethan felt like he was piecing together something far greater than a childhood dream.

By the time the sun dipped low on the horizon, the treehouse had begun to resemble its former glory. The walls were sturdy, the roof patched, and the floorboards secure. It wasn't perfect, but it was theirs.

As they stood back to admire their work, Grace turned to Ethan, a playful smile tugging at her lips. "So, when's the coronation?"

Ethan laughed, the sound full and genuine. "Soon. But first, I've got a throne to build."

Her laughter joined his, and in that moment, standing side by side beneath the old oak tree, Ethan felt something he hadn't in years: peace.

The woodshop smelled of fresh pine and sawdust, a comforting scent that reminded Ethan of his teenage years. The sounds of hammers and tools echoed throughout the room as he and Grace stood side by side, working on the throne that would soon take pride of place in the treehouse. The workshop was spacious, filled with tools that gleamed under the overhead lights, and workbenches lined with half-finished projects.

Grace ran her fingers over a smooth piece of oak, her brow furrowed in concentration. "I think we should make the seat a little wider, give it more of a royal feel," she suggested, glancing at Ethan for approval.

Ethan nodded, his mind still on the conversation they'd had months ago. The words Grace had spoken then, back when they'd first started this journey, echoed in his thoughts: *"You could rebuild it to honor your mom."*

He stood still for a moment, watching her as she sketched out a rough design for the throne, her face illuminated by the soft light in the shop. There was something about the way she moved, how she touched each piece of wood with care, as though the furniture wasn't just something to be built—it was something to be cherished.

That thought triggered something in him—a deep, almost forgotten memory. His mother, Lila, had always been the one to remind him that home wasn't just a place. It was the people you built your life with, the moments you shared, the memories you created. She had been the one to instill in him the value of hard work, the importance of honoring those who came before you.

Suddenly, Ethan felt a rush of clarity. Grace's words, her suggestion to honor his mom, had never felt more meaningful. This treehouse, this project—it wasn't just a way to rebuild his past. It was a way to honor the woman who had given him everything despite the darkness in his life.

He moved toward the stack of wood at the far end of the room, his footsteps heavy with purpose. Grace looked up as he picked out a sturdy piece of walnut. "What are you thinking?" she asked, her eyes curious.

"I want to build something for her," Ethan said, his voice low but steady. "A plaque, something simple, but meaningful. Something to honor her, for everything she gave me."

Grace smiled softly, nodding as she set down her pencil. "I think that's a beautiful idea."

They worked together in silence for a while, Ethan carefully carving the letters into the plaque, his hands steady but his heart heavy with emotion. It wasn't until the sun began to set, casting a warm golden glow through the windows of the shop, that he finally finished. The plaque read:

Lila's Kingdom
Built with love, rebuilt with hope.

Ethan ran his fingers over the smooth surface, feeling the weight of the words. It wasn't much, but it felt right. He could almost hear his mother's voice in his head, urging him to never forget where he came from, to never lose sight of the people who made him who he was.

Grace came over, her gaze soft as she looked at the plaque. "It's perfect, Ethan," she said, her voice thick with emotion. "I know she would've been proud of you."

Ethan's throat tightened as he looked at the words, the weight of the moment settling over him. "I hope so." He paused, taking a deep breath. "This treehouse... this is for her. And for me. For both of us."

Grace nodded, understanding in her eyes. "It's beautiful. And so are you, for doing this."

They stood in silence for a few moments, the weight of the past and the present pressing down on Ethan's chest. The treehouse had started as a way to rebuild the memories of his childhood, but now, it had become something more. It was a symbol of healing, of growth, and of the love he had for the people who had shaped him.

With the plaque in hand, they made their way back to the treehouse, the evening air cool against their skin. Grace carried the plaque carefully, holding it with the same reverence she had when they first began this project. They reached the treehouse, and Ethan climbed the ladder first, extending his hand to Grace. She took it, her fingers warm against his, and together, they placed the plaque at the entrance of the treehouse, a permanent reminder of Lila's love.

Ethan stepped back, gazing at the plaque with a sense of finality. "It's done," he murmured. "The house is truly ours now."

Grace looked at him, her eyes full of understanding and warmth. "No, Ethan. It was always yours. You just needed to claim it."

He turned to face her, the weight of his past slowly lifting. "And now I have." He paused, his heart full. "Thank you, Grace. For everything."

She smiled, her eyes softening as she stepped closer to him. "There's nowhere else I'd rather be."

As the last light of the day slipped behind the horizon, Ethan felt a deep sense of peace settle within him. The past was no longer something to run from. It was a part of him, a part of who he was and who he would continue to become. And in this moment, with Grace by his side, he knew he had finally found his home—both in Ashville and in her heart.

Chapter Nine

Ethan stood in the treehouse, the scent of fresh wood and sawdust filling the air. The transformation was almost complete. He and Grace had worked tirelessly, the space now a perfect blend of nostalgia and hope. The wooden throne sat proudly in its place, and the plaque honoring his mother gleamed in the fading light. The treehouse, once a relic of his childhood, now stood as a testament to his journey—a place where he had grown, healed, and finally found peace.

Grace stood beside him, admiring their work. "It's perfect," she whispered, her voice full of awe. "You did it, Ethan. You really did."

Ethan gazed at the space, the familiar branches reaching for the sky like old friends. "We did it," he corrected her, his heart full. He had come a long way—farther than he had ever imagined—and now, he was ready to fully embrace the life he had built with Grace by his side.

They spent the rest of the evening in the treehouse, reminiscing about the past and making plans for the future. Grace had always been there for him, helping him rebuild more than just a physical structure. She had helped him rebuild his heart.

But just as they were beginning to feel like they had everything they needed, the phone call came.

Ethan's phone vibrated in his pocket, the sound sharp and sudden. He pulled it out, glancing at the screen. The name on the caller ID made his stomach drop.

Maria.

Ethan's heart skipped a beat. Maria had been a lifeline for him during some of his darkest days. The housekeeper who had given him shelter, food, and warmth when he had nowhere else to turn. Over the years, she had become like family. He answered the call quickly, his voice tight with concern.

"Maria, what's wrong?"

Her voice on the other end was shaky, full of anxiety. "Ethan... it's Clara. She's been in an accident. A bad one. She's in the hospital, and they don't think she's going to make it."

Ethan's blood ran cold. Clara. The woman who had taught him so much, the one who had taken him under her wing and given him the chance to build the life he had in Gulf City. The woman who had always been there when he needed her. The thought of losing her now felt unbearable.

"I'm on my way," he said, his voice barely above a whisper.

"Ethan, please—" Maria's voice broke, and he could hear her sobbing softly. "You need to get here. It's urgent. She's asking for you."

The words hit Ethan like a punch to the gut. He knew Clara didn't have much time left. She had been a mother figure to him in many ways, guiding him, offering wisdom when he needed it most. And now, he couldn't imagine losing her.

Without thinking, he turned to Grace, who was standing a few feet away, watching him with concern. Her face fell as she saw the look on his face.

"What's wrong, Ethan?" she asked, her voice quiet but full of worry.

Ethan didn't want to leave her, didn't want to face the possibility of losing Clara. But he knew he had to go.

"Clara's been in an accident. I have to go see her," he said, his voice thick with emotion.

Grace nodded, her gaze soft and understanding. "Of course. You need to be with her."

Ethan grabbed his coat, his heart heavy. "I'll go alone, but I'd like you to come with me, Grace. I need you there... with me. I want you to meet Clara. She's the woman who helped me when I was lost. She's been like a second mother to me, and I need you to meet her."

Grace's eyes softened. She could see the depth of Ethan's feelings for Clara, the way this woman had shaped him, and she understood the importance of this.

"I'll go with you, Ethan," Grace said, her voice steady. "I'll be there for you."

Ethan felt a rush of gratitude toward her. As much as he hated the reason they were going, he felt a sense of peace knowing that Grace was by his side.

The drive to the hospital was filled with an oppressive silence. Ethan's thoughts swirled in a fog of worry and fear, each passing mile feeling like an eternity. He couldn't shake the image of Clara in the hospital bed, fighting for her life. He wanted to believe she would make it, but a part of him feared the worst.

When they arrived, they were directed to a small waiting room. The sterile scent of the hospital filled the air, and Ethan could feel the weight of the situation bearing down on him. He looked at Grace, who stood quietly beside him, her hand lightly resting on his arm.

He squeezed her hand in return, grateful for her presence. She didn't say anything—she didn't need to. She was there for him, and that was enough.

A few minutes later, a nurse appeared, her face grim.

"Mr. Blackwell, Ms. Turner?" she asked.

"Yes," Ethan said, his voice tight. "How is Clara?"

The nurse hesitated before speaking, her words measured. "She's stable for now, but it's not looking good. She's asking for you, Mr. Blackwell."

Ethan's heart clenched. He nodded quickly, following the nurse down the sterile hallway, his mind racing with the possibility that he might be too late.

The door to Clara's room was open, and Ethan stepped inside. Clara lay in the hospital bed, pale and fragile, her once vibrant eyes now clouded with pain. When she saw him, her face softened, a weak but warm smile spreading across her lips.

"Ethan," she whispered, her voice raspy.

He walked to her side, taking her hand in his. "I'm here, Clara. I'm here."

Her smile faded, replaced by a look of sadness. "I didn't think I'd get the chance to see you again, kid," she said, her voice trembling. "I thought I'd lost you for good."

Tears welled in Ethan's eyes, but he forced them back. "You didn't lose me, Clara. I'm here now. And I'll always be here for you."

Clara's gaze flickered to Grace, who was standing in the doorway. Grace stepped forward slowly, her presence calming.

"Grace," Clara said softly, her voice barely a whisper. "I'm glad to meet you. Ethan's told me so much about you."

Grace smiled gently, stepping closer to the bed. "It's an honor to meet you, Clara. Thank you for everything you've done for him."

Clara gave a faint smile. "He's a good man. He's come so far. You've been good for him."

Ethan looked at Clara, his heart heavy. "I'm not going anywhere. I promise you that."

Clara squeezed his hand, her eyes soft with understanding. "I know you're not. Just... don't let the past hold you back, Ethan. You've found your place. You've found your people."

Ethan nodded, feeling the weight of her words settle deep in his chest.

Before long, Clara fell into a fitful sleep, and Ethan and Grace were left alone in the quiet room. Grace reached for his hand, her grip steady.

"Ethan, I want you to know that no matter what happens, I'm here. You don't have to go through this alone."

Ethan's heart swelled with gratitude. "I don't know what I'd do without you."

They sat in the quiet hospital room, holding onto each other as the hours stretched on, knowing that life would never be the same again.

The funeral was held in a quiet, secluded cemetery on the outskirts of Gulf City. The sky was overcast, a gentle drizzle of rain misting the air as mourners gathered around Clara's grave. The crowd was larger than Ethan had expected, with people from all walks of life showing up to pay their respects. The friends, customers, and employees who had known Clara for years were there, each one touched by the mark she had left on their lives.

Ethan stood at the front, just behind Clara's casket, his heart heavy. The grief he felt was deep, but it was also tinged with gratitude. Clara had been a guide, a mentor, and a friend—more family than anything else. The ache in his chest was undeniable, but beneath it was a quiet strength, one that he knew Clara would have been proud of.

Grace stood by his side, offering a steadying hand. She had been with him through everything—his journey back to Ashville, the rebuilding of his life, and now, the loss of someone who had meant so much to him.

As the crowd murmured their goodbyes, Ethan couldn't help but notice the faces in the crowd—some old, some new. Familiar faces from his past, the ones who had watched him grow from a boy with little direction into the man he was today. Joe was there, standing off to the side with his cap pulled low over his face. Maria, her eyes red from crying, stood next to him, holding his hand. She had been Clara's dear friend, and her heartache was palpable.

Ethan met Joe's gaze across the cemetery, and the older man nodded in acknowledgment, his expression solemn but proud. He had been a part of Ethan's journey from the very beginning, always offering quiet wisdom and a safe space. Without Joe, and without Maria, he wasn't sure where he'd be.

Maria's gaze found his, and she made her way over, her footsteps slow and deliberate. She stood beside him, her arms open, ready to embrace him in the way only a mother could.

"You've grown into someone I'm so proud of, Ethan," Maria said quietly, her voice thick with emotion. "Clara would have been proud too. She always knew you'd be something great."

Ethan swallowed hard, blinking away the tears that threatened to fall. "Thank you, Maria," he whispered. "I don't think I would have made it without you or Clara. I owe everything to you both."

Maria smiled softly, squeezing his shoulder. "You don't owe me anything. You've earned it all, Ethan. You've done more than just rebuild yourself; you've rebuilt this town."

Her words stung deep, and Ethan felt the weight of them more than ever. The people of Gulf City, people who had given him a second chance, now saw him for who he truly was. The boy who had once been lost was now a man with purpose, a man who had learned from his mistakes and forged his own path.

As the funeral procession continued, Ethan found himself lost in thought. He had come so far, but there was still so much left to do.

After the ceremony, the mourners gathered at a small reception hall nearby, a place where people could share stories and memories of Clara. It was a bittersweet time, full of laughter and tears, as old friends and former colleagues came together to honor the woman who had given so much to the community.

Ethan sat at the back of the room, nursing a glass of water, when he noticed several familiar faces approaching. He recognized them as old customers—people who had supported him and Clara's business for years, but who had also known him in the dark days before he had truly found his place in the world.

"Ethan," one of them said, a broad smile on his face. "We knew you had it in you, kid. You've come a long way."

Ethan stood and shook the man's hand, his voice thick with gratitude. "Thank you. I wouldn't be here without the support of people like you."

The small crowd around him nodded in agreement, each one sharing stories about Clara's impact on their lives. The air was thick with emotion, but it was also full of a quiet joy—a celebration of the woman who had shaped so many lives, including Ethan's.

As the conversations shifted, Maria made her way over, Joe close behind her. She pulled Ethan into a tight hug, her sobs muffled against his chest.

"I'm so sorry, Maria," Ethan whispered, his own emotions bubbling up once more. "She was like family to me."

Maria pulled back, wiping her eyes. "I know she was. She always saw something in you, Ethan. She knew you were destined for great things."

Joe clapped Ethan on the back, his strong hands firm and reassuring. "She wasn't wrong," he said with a smile that didn't quite reach his eyes. "You've done everything we all knew you could. You've built something that matters, Ethan. We're all proud of you."

Grace had been watching from a distance, her own emotions quiet but present. She saw the way the people from his past looked at him, saw the pride and admiration in their eyes. She felt the weight of it all—the love, the support, the shared history.

She walked over, gently taking Ethan's hand in hers. "You've come a long way, haven't you?" she said softly.

Ethan nodded, his heart full. "I wouldn't have made it here without you, Grace. I need you to know that. Every step of the way, you've been with me. I can't imagine doing this without you."

Grace smiled warmly, her thumb brushing the back of his hand. "I'm not going anywhere, Ethan. I'm here. And no matter what happens next, we'll figure it out together."

As the day wore on, Ethan found himself surrounded by people who had been a part of his journey. They had watched him grow from a boy who didn't know where he was headed into a man who had found his purpose. But it wasn't just the work he had done in Gulf City that had earned their respect—it was the man he had become.

As the final moments of the funeral faded, and people began to trickle out, Ethan felt a profound sense of peace settle over him. He had lost Clara, but he had gained so much in the process. The lessons she had taught him, the love she had shown him, would never fade.

He turned to Grace, and for the first time in a long while, he felt like he was exactly where he was meant to be. With her.

As the last of the mourners began to leave, the reception hall grew quieter. Ethan lingered by the entrance, shaking hands and sharing words of comfort with those who approached him. It felt surreal—being the one others leaned on, the one who now represented Clara's legacy. He hadn't realized how deeply rooted her presence was in the lives of so many.

Maria and Joe stayed behind to help clean up. Grace moved around the room, stacking plates and cups onto a tray. She worked silently, occasionally glancing at Ethan as he spoke with yet another old acquaintance. There was a softness to her gaze, a mixture of pride and quiet concern.

When the hall was nearly empty, Maria approached Ethan again. Her face was calm, but her voice trembled slightly.

"Ethan," she said, "I want to thank you for what you did for Clara—for being there when she needed you most. She always talked about you like you were her own son. And I think, in a way, you were."

Her words caught him off guard, and he felt his throat tighten. "She meant the world to me," he said, his voice barely above a whisper. "I wouldn't be who I am without her."

Maria smiled, a glimmer of warmth breaking through her grief. "She knew that. And I think she'd want you to know that it's okay to grieve her, but it's also okay to move forward. Clara was never one to dwell on things, and she wouldn't want you to either."

Joe chimed in, his deep voice steady. "She always said you had more work to do, Ethan. That you weren't done yet. And judging by the woman standing over there watching you, I'd say she was right."

Ethan turned his head slightly, following Joe's gaze to Grace, who had just finished clearing a table. She caught his eye and gave him a small smile, her cheeks flushing as she looked away.

Joe clapped Ethan on the shoulder. "You're a good man, Ethan. Don't let anything—or anyone—convince you otherwise."

As Joe and Maria headed out, Ethan walked over to Grace, who was now wiping down one of the last tables. He hesitated for a moment before speaking.

"You didn't have to do all this," he said softly.

Grace shrugged, setting the rag down. "I wanted to help. Besides, I know how much Clara meant to you. I couldn't just sit back and watch."

Ethan leaned against the table, his hands in his pockets. "You've always been there for me, Grace. Even when I didn't deserve it."

She looked at him, her expression gentle but firm. "You deserve more than you give yourself credit for, Ethan. Clara saw that, and so do I."

Her words lingered in the air, heavy with meaning. Ethan wanted to respond, but the weight of the day, the emotions of saying goodbye to Clara, and the presence of Grace by his side rendered him speechless.

Instead, he reached out and took her hand. Grace didn't pull away. She stepped closer, resting her head against his shoulder, and they stood there in silence, letting the moment speak for itself.

Later that evening, Ethan and Grace found themselves driving through Gulf City. Ethan had wanted to show her a few of the places that had been important to him during his time there.

"This is where it all started," Ethan said as he pulled up to the food truck lot where he'd met Joe all those years ago. The spot was nearly empty now, just a few scattered trucks still open for late-night customers.

He pointed to a corner near the edge of the lot. "That's where I sat when I didn't have a dollar to my name. Joe handed me a sandwich and told me not to worry about it. He didn't know me, didn't owe me anything, but he helped me anyway."

Grace looked at him, her expression thoughtful. "It seems like a lot of people saw something in you before you saw it in yourself."

Ethan nodded, his gaze distant. "Yeah. I guess I've been lucky that way. Joe, Maria, Clara...they all gave me chances I didn't think I deserved."

Grace reached out and placed a hand on his arm. "They saw who you were, Ethan. The same way I always did."

Her words hit him harder than he expected, and he found himself blinking away tears. He cleared his throat and started the car again, pulling away from the lot.

Their final stop was Clara's workshop. Ethan parked the car and got out, the familiar sight of the building bringing a wave of bittersweet memories. He unlocked the door and led Grace inside, flipping on the lights to reveal the organized chaos that had always defined Clara's workspace.

"She taught me everything here," Ethan said, his voice tinged with reverence. "Not just about furniture, but about life. She showed me what it meant to work hard, to care about what you're creating."

Grace wandered through the workshop, running her fingers over the sanded edges of an unfinished chair. "You've come so far, Ethan. And I think Clara would be so proud of the man you've become."

Ethan stepped closer, his heart full. "I couldn't have done it without you, Grace. You've always been my anchor, even when I didn't realize it."

Grace turned to him, her eyes shining. "And I always will be."

The moment hung between them, unspoken words filling the space. Ethan reached out, pulling Grace into an embrace, and for the first time in a long time, he felt like he was exactly where he was meant to be.

The drive back to Ashville was quieter than the trip to Gulf City had been. Ethan kept one hand on the steering wheel, the other resting idly on the gear shift. Grace sat beside him, gazing out at the scenery as it shifted from the urban sprawl of Gulf City to the rolling hills and wooded outskirts of Ashville.

Ethan's mind was a whirlwind. Clara's funeral had dredged up emotions he hadn't expected—grief, of course, but also clarity. Seeing the people who had shaped his life, who had believed in him, reminded him of the path he'd walked to get to this moment. And now, as the small town he once called home came into view, he couldn't ignore the quiet tug in his chest.

Ashville wasn't just a place anymore. It wasn't just the town he'd left behind. It was Grace. It was the home he was rebuilding, the treehouse they'd restored together. It was a new beginning, but the weight of that realization sat heavy in his chest. Could he really build a future here?

When they arrived back in town, Ethan parked the car in front of the house. The sight of the newly restored exterior, gleaming in the late afternoon sun, brought a flicker of pride. It looked nothing like the shell of a home he'd walked into months ago.

Grace stepped out, stretching her arms and inhaling the fresh, familiar air. "It's good to be back," she said, flashing Ethan a warm smile.

He nodded, joining her on the porch. "It feels...different this time," he admitted, his voice soft.

Grace tilted her head, studying him. "Different how?"

Ethan hesitated. "Like it's not just a place I'm passing through. Like it could really be home."

Grace didn't respond right away. Instead, she reached for his hand, lacing her fingers through his. "Maybe it always was," she said gently.

Her words lingered in Ethan's mind as they stepped inside. The house was quiet, but it felt alive in a way it hadn't before. They spent the rest of the afternoon sketching plans for the future. Ethan talked about expanding his workshop, maybe offering apprenticeships to local craftsmen. Grace chimed in with ideas for community involvement, hosting events, and turning the business into something that could truly benefit the town.

"We could start small," Grace suggested. "Focus on custom pieces for people around here, and then branch out. You've already got connections in Gulf City; they could help spread the word."

Ethan nodded, a small smile playing on his lips. "You make it sound so easy."

Grace laughed. "It won't be. But nothing worth doing ever is."

That night, Ethan found himself alone in the living room. Grace had gone home to shower and change, promising to return in the morning to finalize more plans. The house was quiet, save for the occasional creak of the floorboards and the soft hum of the wind outside.

Ethan sat on the couch, staring at the coffee table where an old family photo rested. It was one he'd found during the restoration process—a picture of his mother, Lila, standing in the garden with a young Ethan by her side. She was smiling, her hands covered in dirt, and Ethan looked up at her with wide, adoring eyes.

He ran a hand through his hair, the weight of his thoughts pressing down on him.

This house, this town, Grace—everything was pulling him toward a future he hadn't dared to imagine. But the fears still lingered. What if he wasn't enough? What if he became like his father—bitter, broken, and incapable of holding on to the things that mattered?

Clara's voice echoed in his mind. *"The threads of fate will always lead you where you need to go."*

But was this where he needed to go? Or was it just where he wanted to be?

Ethan leaned back, closing his eyes. Images of Clara, Maria, Joe, and Grace swirled in his mind, each of them representing a part of his journey. They had all believed in him, even when he hadn't believed in himself. And now, for the first time, he wanted to believe too.

The next morning, Ethan and Grace stood in the yard, looking up at the treehouse. The final touches had been completed, and the new wooden plaque honoring his mother hung proudly by the entrance.

Grace turned to Ethan, her expression soft. "So, what's next?"

Ethan looked at her, his heart swelling with a mix of fear and hope. "We keep building," he said simply.

Grace smiled, reaching for his hand. "Together?"

"Together," Ethan replied, his voice steady.

As they stood there, the sun rising over the trees, Ethan felt the weight of his fears begin to lift. For the first time in years, he wasn't running away. He was standing still, ready to face whatever came next.

Chapter Ten

Ethan and Grace stood outside the old hardware store in the heart of Ashville's town square. The once modest building that Ethan transformed into his workshop now buzzes with potential. Its large windows showcased Ethan's carefully crafted furniture pieces, drawing the attention of passersby. The familiar scent of sawdust mixed with the crisp morning air as Ethan unlocked the door.

Inside, Grace joined him at the workbench, sketchpads spread out before them. They had spent weeks planning the expansion. The space, while cozy and functional, was no longer sufficient to accommodate the growing demand for Ethan's work. They envisioned a workshop bustling with employees, each corner alive with creativity and craftsmanship.

Grace tapped a pencil against her chin as she studied the layout Ethan had drawn. "So, if we knock down this wall," she said, pointing to the back of the building, "we could add a storage room here. That way, we won't be tripping over supplies every time a big order comes in."

Ethan nodded, his brow furrowed as he considered her suggestion. "And maybe here," he gestured toward another part of the sketch, "we could add a small showroom. Something to showcase finished pieces for clients who stop by."

Grace's eyes lit up. "Exactly! This could be more than just a workshop—it could be the heart of Ashville's craftsmanship."

As they brainstormed, Ethan couldn't help but marvel at how seamlessly Grace had become part of this dream. She was not just his partner in life but now his partner in business, too. Her ideas were practical and innovative, complementing his vision perfectly.

Later that afternoon, they met with a contractor in the square. Ethan explained his ideas, gesturing animatedly toward the building while Grace filled in the details. The contractor listened intently, nodding along and occasionally jotting down notes.

"This is doable," the contractor said finally. "We can have the renovations started by next month, assuming permits go through quickly."

Ethan glanced at Grace, who gave him an encouraging nod. "Let's do it," Ethan said firmly, shaking the contractor's hand.

With the plans for expansion in motion, Ethan and Grace celebrated with lunch at a small café nearby. The town square was bustling with life—children playing on the fountain's edge, shopkeepers greeting customers, and the warm hum of a community Ethan had once thought he'd left behind forever.

As they sat together, Ethan felt a wave of contentment, but beneath it was a flicker of uncertainty. He couldn't shake the thought that things were moving too quickly. Was he truly ready for this?

Grace must have noticed his quietness because she reached across the table, taking his hand in hers. "Hey," she said softly, "we're doing this together, remember? Whatever you're feeling—we'll figure it out."

Ethan looked at her, his heart tightening. Grace's steady presence was a balm to his restless thoughts. "I know," he said finally. "It's just... a lot to take in. Expanding the workshop, planning our future—it feels like everything is happening at once."

She smiled, her eyes warm. "That's because we're building something real, Ethan. Something worth every bit of effort."

Her words settled something inside him. Ethan squeezed her hand. "You're right. I couldn't do this without you."

The rest of the day passed in a flurry of activity—finalizing plans, ordering materials, and sketching out the next steps. By the time they locked up the workshop that evening, the building felt alive with possibility.

As they walked home through the square, Grace looped her arm through Ethan's. "So," she said with a teasing grin, "do I get to be the boss when this place really takes off?"

Ethan chuckled. "You already are."

Over the next few weeks, the workshop became a hub of energy and anticipation. Contractors began arriving early each morning, their trucks lining the narrow streets of the town square. The sound of hammers and saws filled the air as walls were knocked down and new spaces began to take shape. Ethan and Grace were there every day, overseeing the progress and pitching in wherever they could.

Grace often found herself stepping into a natural leadership role. She coordinated with the contractors, organized schedules, and ensured the project stayed on track. Ethan admired her ability to take charge. She seemed to thrive under the pressure, her determination driving the project forward.

One evening, after the contractors had left for the day, Ethan and Grace lingered in the workshop. Dust hung in the air, and the warm glow of the setting sun filtered through the half-finished showroom windows. Ethan ran his hand over a newly installed beam, marveling at the progress.

"It's really happening," he said, a mix of pride and disbelief in his voice.

Grace leaned against the workbench, arms crossed and a small smile playing on her lips. "It is. And it's going to be incredible."

Ethan walked over to her, brushing a stray speck of sawdust from her cheek. "I don't say this enough, but thank you. For everything. For believing in this... in me."

She looked up at him, her eyes soft. "Ethan, you've built something amazing—not just here, but in this town, in us. I'm just lucky to be a part of it."

They stood there in the quiet workshop, the weight of their journey together settling between them. It wasn't just a workshop they were building—it was a life, a future, a promise.

As the weeks turned into months, the project neared completion. The new showroom was a masterpiece, with wide windows that showcased Ethan's work and an open floor plan that allowed customers to see the craftsmanship up close. The storage room solved a problem Ethan hadn't realized was weighing on him, and the expanded workspace buzzed with potential for the team he and Grace were beginning to assemble.

On the day the renovations were finally complete, the town square seemed to come alive in celebration. Neighbors stopped by to admire the transformation, offering their congratulations and sharing stories about the old hardware store's history.

Ethan and Grace hosted an informal open house that evening, inviting friends, townsfolk, and even the contractors who had worked tirelessly to bring the vision to life. The shop was filled with laughter and the sound of clinking glasses as people admired the furniture and the space itself.

Joe, the food truck owner who had fed Ethan when he first arrived in Gulf City, was among the guests. He gave Ethan a hearty slap on the back. "You've come a long way, kid. This is something to be proud of."

Maria stood nearby, her eyes glistening as she admired the space. "Clara would've loved this," she said softly, and Ethan felt a pang of bittersweet emotion. He nodded, his voice thick as he replied, "I hope so."

Later that night, after the guests had left and the workshop was quiet again, Ethan and Grace stood in the showroom. The moonlight streamed through the windows, casting soft shadows across the polished floor.

Ethan turned to Grace, taking her hand. "This place—it's not just a workshop anymore. It's a second chance. For me, for us, for everything I thought I'd lost."

Grace squeezed his hand, her voice steady. "And it's ours now. Together."

For the first time in a long while, Ethan felt truly at peace. Ashville wasn't just his home—it was his future.

The next morning, sunlight poured through the wide windows of the newly renovated workshop, casting a warm glow over the tools and materials neatly arranged on the workbenches. Ethan and Grace had made a habit of arriving early, savoring the quiet before the day's work began.

Grace was at her station, sanding the edge of a table she had taken on as a side project. Ethan worked on a detailed sketch for a custom dining set requested by a client. The sound of sandpaper rasping against wood and the scratch of Ethan's pencil created a comforting rhythm.

"Hey," Grace said, breaking the silence. She brushed a stray strand of hair from her face, leaving a faint streak of sawdust on her cheek. "What do you think about this?" She held up the table's corner, now smoothed and rounded with a delicate curve.

Ethan looked up, a smile tugging at his lips. "You've got an eye for details, you know that?"

She grinned, setting the table leg down. "Well, I've had a pretty good teacher."

They worked in companionable silence for a while, the air between them warm with the easy rapport they had developed. But as the hours passed and the light in the workshop shifted, Grace's demeanor seemed to change. She hesitated before speaking, her voice careful.

"Ethan, can I ask you something?" she said, her sanding block still in her hand.

"Of course," he said, glancing up from his sketch.

She set the sanding block down, leaning against the workbench. "Where do you see us in a few years? What do you think this"—she gestured between them—"looks like down the line?"

Ethan froze for a moment, caught off guard by the question. He set his pencil down, leaning back in his chair. "I haven't really thought about it," he lied, his heart pounding. "I mean, I have, but not... in detail."

Grace tilted her head, studying him. "Ethan, come on. I know you. You've always got plans and backup plans. What's on your mind?"

He sighed, running a hand through his hair. "I don't know, Grace. I think about it—us, the future—but sometimes it feels... overwhelming."

She nodded slowly, her expression patient but searching. "Why overwhelming? What's holding you back?"

Ethan hesitated. The truth felt too big, too tangled to articulate. But Grace's steady gaze gave him the courage to try.

"It's not that I don't want it," he began, his voice low. "I do. I think about a life with you—marriage, kids, everything. But every time I start to picture it, I feel this... weight. Like I'm afraid I'll mess it up. That I'll end up like my dad, or worse, that I'll fail you in some other way."

Grace's face softened, and she took a step closer. "Ethan, you're not your father. You've proven that in everything you've done—in the way you treat people, the way you've turned your life around."

"I know that," Ethan said, his voice rough. "Logically, I know. But there's this part of me that keeps whispering, 'What if?' What if I'm not enough? What if I can't give you the life you deserve?"

Grace reached for his hand, holding it tightly. "Ethan, you've already given me so much. I don't need some perfect life or perfect version of you. I just need you—flaws, fears, and all."

Her words settled over him like a balm, but the knot in his chest didn't fully untangle. He looked down at their joined hands, his thumb brushing over hers. "I just want to make sure I'm ready. That I can be the person you need me to be."

Grace smiled softly. "The fact that you're worried about that already tells me you're the right person. But I also know this is something you need to figure out for yourself. Just know that I'm here, Ethan. I'm not going anywhere."

The workshop felt quieter than it had all morning as the weight of their conversation lingered. Ethan squeezed her hand, his mind racing with thoughts of what his future with Grace could look like—and the fears that still clung to him.

A few months later, the workshop was buzzing with life and activity. The once quiet and solitary space Ethan and Grace had shared now echoed with the sounds of tools humming, laughter, and the steady murmur of collaboration.

Three new employees worked alongside them—a mix of fresh-faced dreamers and experienced woodworkers eager to expand their craft. Grace stood at one of the larger tables, guiding a young designer named Lily through a sketch. Lily had a keen eye for detail, but her confidence wavered when translating her ideas to paper.

"See here?" Grace said, pointing to a curved line on the sketchpad. "This is good, but it could flow more naturally into the next section. Try softening the angle and think about how the wood will respond when Ethan starts shaping it."

Lily nodded, her pencil moving cautiously across the page. "Like this?"

"Exactly," Grace said, her smile warm. "You're getting it. Keep going."

Across the room, Ethan worked with Mason, a burly man in his mid-thirties who was new to woodworking but showed an innate talent for the craft. Ethan watched as Mason carefully ran a piece of walnut through the planer, his hands steady but unsure.

"You're pressing too hard," Ethan said, stepping closer. "Let the machine do the work. You just guide it."

Mason adjusted his grip, and the planer hummed as the wood came out smooth and even. He held it up, his face lighting up with pride. "That's a lot better."

"Perfect," Ethan said with a nod. "Keep practicing that technique. Once you get the feel for it, you'll be able to tackle more complex pieces."

Ethan glanced across the room, his eyes landing on Grace. She was laughing at something Lily had said, her whole demeanor radiant as she encouraged the younger woman. He couldn't help but smile. They had built this together—a space that wasn't just a business but a place for people to learn, grow, and create.

By lunchtime, the employees were gathered around a makeshift table they had cobbled together out of spare wood—a tradition Grace had started to foster camaraderie. Ethan sat at the head, watching as Mason cracked a joke that sent everyone into fits of laughter.

As the meal wound down, Ethan tapped his glass with his fork, the sound cutting through the chatter. "Hey, before everyone gets back to work, I just want to say something."

The group quieted, all eyes on him.

"When Grace and I decided to expand this workshop, we had no idea what it would turn into. But seeing all of you here, working together and bringing your ideas to life, it's more than I could have hoped for. This place isn't just about furniture—it's about building something bigger than ourselves. And I'm grateful to have each of you here for that."

The room erupted into applause, and Ethan caught Grace's eye. She gave him a small nod, her expression filled with pride.

As the afternoon wore on, Ethan found himself working with a young apprentice named Tyler, who had just joined the new apprenticeship program. Tyler was eager but rough around the edges, his enthusiasm often outpacing his skill.

"Let's start simple," Ethan said, showing Tyler how to carve a basic joint. "It's not about speed; it's about precision. Take your time."

Tyler nodded, his brow furrowed in concentration as he worked. Ethan watched, offering pointers and encouragement, and gradually, Tyler's confidence grew.

By the end of the day, the workshop quieted as the employees trickled out, leaving Ethan and Grace alone. They stood side by side, surveying the space that had transformed so much over the past few months.

"It's amazing, isn't it?" Grace said softly. "What we've built here."

"It is," Ethan replied, his voice filled with awe. "I never thought I'd have this—something that feels so... permanent."

Grace looked up at him, her eyes shining. "And it's only the beginning."

Ethan smiled, but her words carried a weight he couldn't ignore. The future stretched out before them, filled with possibility, and for the first time, he allowed himself to believe it could truly be theirs.

Chapter Eleven

Ethan leaned back in his chair, the faint glow of his laptop illuminating his tired face. The workshop office was silent, save for the faint hum of the air conditioning and the occasional buzz of his phone. Stacks of papers cluttered the desk—blueprints, invoices, and a growing list of contracts from his Gulf City connections. The business was booming, expanding far beyond what he and Grace had originally imagined.

For the past few weeks, Ethan had been juggling calls with manufacturers, setting up meetings, and coordinating shipments. The contracts coming in were no small feats—galleries, corporate offices, even high-end furniture retailers in larger cities. Each deal brought new opportunities, but also more stress and longer hours.

Grace knocked lightly on the office door, peeking her head in. "You're still at it?"

Ethan glanced at the clock on his computer screen—9:47 PM. He sighed, rubbing the back of his neck. "Yeah. Just trying to finalize this proposal for that gallery in Charleston."

She stepped inside, carrying a mug of coffee. "You've been at it all day. Maybe you should call it a night."

"I can't," he said, shaking his head. "If I don't get this out tonight, we might lose the deal."

Grace set the mug on his desk, her brow furrowed. "You've been saying that a lot lately."

Ethan paused, the weight of her words sinking in. He leaned forward, resting his elbows on the desk. "I know. I just... I can't let this slip. This is what we've been working for, right? Expanding, making a name for ourselves?"

She crossed her arms, her voice quieter now. "It's what *you've* been working for. I'm starting to wonder if you even see me in the picture anymore."

Ethan looked up, his heart sinking. "That's not fair, Grace. You know how much this means to me—to *us*."

"But at what cost?" she asked, her voice breaking slightly. "You're so focused on building this empire that you're forgetting why we started this in the first place. It wasn't about contracts or galleries in Charleston. It was about creating something meaningful, together."

He stared at her, at the hurt in her eyes, and felt an ache in his chest. She was right, but admitting that felt like betraying the progress he'd made. "I'm doing this for us," he said softly. "For the future we talked about."

"No, Ethan," Grace said, shaking her head. "*I* talked about a future. About marriage, about building a family. You haven't said a word about any of that since we started this expansion."

He opened his mouth to respond, but the words caught in his throat. The truth was, the thought of marriage and children terrified him. Every time the idea crept into his mind, he was flooded with memories of his father—the anger, the disappointment, the fear that he'd somehow repeat the cycle.

Grace sighed, stepping closer. "I'm not asking you to drop everything, Ethan. I'm just asking you to find a balance. To show me that I matter as much as this business."

"You *do* matter," he said quickly, reaching for her hand. "More than anything."

"Then show me," she whispered, her voice trembling. "Because right now, it doesn't feel that way."

She pulled her hand back, leaving him alone in the dimly lit office. Ethan sat there, the silence heavier than before. He stared at the coffee mug she'd brought, now cooling on the desk, and felt the weight of her words pressing down on him.

The next morning, Ethan tried to shake off the lingering tension. He threw himself into the workshop, directing employees and reviewing new designs. But even as he worked, Grace's words echoed in his mind.

Later that day, an email notification popped up on his phone—another potential contract from a furniture distributor in New York City. It was a game-changer, the kind of opportunity he'd dreamed of. But as he stared at the screen, the excitement he normally felt was replaced by a gnawing sense of unease.

Grace walked into the workshop, her presence grounding him. She was talking to Lily and Mason, her smile warm and genuine, but Ethan noticed the way her eyes didn't meet his. He felt the distance between them growing, like a widening crack in the foundation of everything they'd built.

That evening, Ethan sat on the porch of his house, a glass of whiskey in his hand. The stars were bright overhead, the night quiet except for the occasional rustle of leaves. He thought about his father, about the life he'd left behind in Gulf City, and about Grace.

He wanted to make her happy, to give her everything she deserved. But the fear of failing her, of not being enough, gnawed at him.

Grace sat on the edge of the bed, staring at her reflection in the mirror across the room. The soft lamplight highlighted the weariness in her face, the small creases on her forehead etched deeper than she remembered. She tucked a strand of hair behind her ear and sighed, her gaze drifting to the empty space beside her on the bed.

Ethan was still at the workshop.

She'd grown used to the hum of the house without him, the quiet evenings that stretched into lonely nights. In the beginning, she'd told herself it was temporary, a necessary phase for their business to grow. But as the weeks turned into months, the ache in her chest grew heavier, more persistent.

Sliding her hands into her lap, Grace thought back to the day they'd sat under the old oak tree, the day he'd carved her name into the wooden throne they built together. That moment had felt like a promise—a sign that they were building something meaningful, not just in their business but in their lives.

She wanted to believe in that promise. She wanted to trust that Ethan's heart was in the same place as hers. But lately, she couldn't ignore the distance between them.

Grace stood, her feet carrying her to the window overlooking the quiet street. She pulled back the curtain and looked out, hoping to see the glow of Ethan's truck headlights. The night was still, and the realization hit her again—he was still chasing something. Something bigger than this town, bigger than her.

It wasn't just the late nights at the workshop or the endless phone calls. It was the way he avoided her questions about the future, the way he deflected every time she brought up marriage or children. Grace felt like she was holding her breath, waiting for him to see her, to really see what she needed.

But what if he never did?

The thought brought a lump to her throat. She sat back down, clasping her hands tightly as if the act could steady the storm brewing inside her.

She loved him. She loved the way he smiled when he thought no one was looking, the way he brought life to the simplest pieces of wood with his hands. She loved the man he'd become, the way he cared for others, the way he tried so hard to make something of himself.

But she couldn't help wondering if he truly saw a future with her. Or if she was just another piece of his past he was trying to fix, like the treehouse or the workshop.

Grace rested her head in her hands, her mind wandering back to their conversation in the office the night before. She'd seen the guilt in his eyes, the way he flinched at her words. He cared—she didn't doubt that. But care wasn't enough. Not anymore.

She wanted a life with him, a real life. She wanted to wake up beside him every morning, to hear the sound of tiny feet running through the house, to feel the warmth of his hand in hers as they grew old together.

But Ethan was a man tethered to his past, and no matter how hard she tried, she couldn't pull him into the future she dreamed of.

A knock at the front door startled her. Grace's heart jumped, and for a moment, she let herself hope it was Ethan. She hurried to the door and opened it to find Lily standing on the porch, a concerned look on her face.

"Hey," Lily said softly. "I just thought I'd check in. You seemed... distracted today."

Grace forced a smile and stepped aside, letting her friend in. "I'm fine. Just... a lot on my mind."

Lily gave her a knowing look as she sat on the couch. "Is it Ethan?"

Grace sat beside her, staring at her hands. "It's always Ethan."

Lily didn't say anything for a moment, and then she reached over, squeezing Grace's hand. "You've been through a lot with him. I know you love him, but... are you happy?"

The question hit Grace like a punch to the chest. She opened her mouth to answer, but the words wouldn't come. Was she happy?

"I don't know," Grace admitted, her voice barely above a whisper. "I want to be. I really do. But he's so caught up in everything else that I don't know if there's room for me in his life anymore."

Lily nodded, her expression thoughtful. "You deserve to be happy, Grace. And you deserve someone who makes you feel like you're their first choice, not their backup plan."

Grace felt tears sting her eyes, but she blinked them away. "I know. But I don't want to give up on him. Not yet."

"Then don't," Lily said gently. "But make sure he knows what's at stake. Don't let him take you for granted."

Grace nodded, her resolve hardening. She wasn't ready to walk away, but she also couldn't keep waiting forever. Ethan needed to figure out what he wanted—and soon.

As the night stretched on, Grace found herself thinking not just about Ethan, but about herself. About the life she wanted, the woman she wanted to be.

And for the first time in a long time, she realized that her happiness wasn't just tied to Ethan's decisions. It was tied to her own.

Ethan leaned over his workbench, the soft whirr of a sanding machine filling the air as he smoothed the edges of a new commission piece. The workshop was alive with the rhythm of productivity—saws buzzing, wood clattering, and muted conversations between employees. It should have felt like an accomplishment, but instead, it felt like a storm he couldn't quite get ahead of.

He glanced toward the design table where Grace sat with one of the apprentices, her face lit by the soft glow of a desk lamp. She was explaining something, her hands moving animatedly as the apprentice nodded along. She laughed at something the young man said, her voice carrying across the workshop.

Ethan felt a tug in his chest. It wasn't jealousy, not exactly—it was guilt.

He turned back to his work, his hands moving on autopilot. The problem wasn't Grace. The problem was him.

Lately, every conversation with her felt like walking a tightrope, and he was always one wrong step away from falling. She'd been patient—more patient than he deserved—but he could feel her patience running out.

He wasn't blind to the tension between them. He'd seen the flicker of disappointment in her eyes when he'd brushed off her questions about marriage. He'd felt the weight of her silence when he came home late, her presence like a shadow that lingered but never spoke.

Ethan straightened and ran a hand through his hair, exhaling sharply. He wanted to fix it. He wanted to tell her that he thought about it, too—that he thought about it all the time. But every time he tried, the words caught in his throat.

What if he wasn't good enough?

What if he couldn't be the husband and father she deserved?

He'd seen firsthand what happened when a man failed his family. He could still hear his father's voice, sharp and slurred, laced with bitterness. He could still see his mother's quiet strength eroding under the weight of broken promises.

What if he was his father's son after all?

"Ethan."

He startled at the sound of Grace's voice and turned to find her standing a few feet away, her arms crossed and a concerned look on her face.

"Hey," he said, setting down the sander. "Everything okay?"

She nodded but didn't move closer. "I was going to ask you the same thing. You've been quiet all day."

Ethan hesitated, the weight of his thoughts pressing down on him. "Just... a lot on my mind. Trying to stay on top of things."

Grace studied him for a moment, her eyes searching his. "You don't have to do it all on your own, you know. That's why we have a team now."

"I know," he said quickly, almost defensively. "It's just... the contracts we're taking on, the deadlines... It's a lot of pressure."

Grace stepped closer, her expression softening. "I get that. I really do. But you've been distant, Ethan. It's like you're here, but you're not really *here*."

Ethan looked away, guilt gnawing at his stomach. "I'm sorry. I don't mean to be."

She reached out, placing a hand on his arm. "I'm not mad. I just... I miss you. The you who carved my name into that throne, who saw this place as more than just work."

Her words hit him like a punch to the gut. He covered her hand with his, squeezing gently. "I miss that, too."

They stood there for a moment, the noise of the workshop fading into the background. Ethan wanted to tell her everything—that he thought about their future, that he wanted it more than anything. But the words felt too big, too heavy.

"I'm trying, Grace," he said finally. "I just... I need time."

Her eyes searched his, and for a moment, he thought she might say something, push him for more. But instead, she nodded, her hand slipping away.

"I know," she said softly. "I just hope you figure out what you want before it's too late."

She turned and walked back to the design table, leaving Ethan alone with his thoughts.

He stared after her, his chest tight. The truth was, he already knew what he wanted. He just didn't know how to get out of his own way.

Ethan lingered by the workbench long after Grace walked away. The hum of the workshop carried on around him, but it was all muted, a backdrop to the chaos in his mind. Her words echoed in his head, carving deeper into him than he wanted to admit.

Figure out what you want before it's too late.

He sank onto a stool, elbows on his knees, and stared down at his hands. They were calloused and steady—hands that had built a life he was proud of. A life that should've been enough.

But was it?

He thought back to the early days of the workshop, the long hours spent repairing chairs and tables, pouring his heart into every piece. Back then, it had been more than just work—it had been a way to prove himself, to show the world he could be something other than a Blackwell with a chip on his shoulder and a reputation to outrun.

And Grace had been there through all of it, reminding him of who he was before the world got in the way.

Now, it felt like he was slipping back into old patterns, letting the pressure consume him, pushing away the one person who made all of this mean something.

Ethan leaned back, running a hand through his hair. The worst part was knowing she was right. He had been distant. He'd buried himself in work, using the contracts and deadlines as an excuse to avoid the bigger questions looming over them both.

Questions like: What did their future look like?

Could he really give her the life she deserved?

The fear gnawed at him, a familiar weight in his chest. He'd seen how love could unravel, how good intentions could curdle into resentment. His parents' marriage had started with love, too. But somewhere along the way, it had fallen apart, leaving behind nothing but anger and regret.

What if I can't be the man she needs?

He exhaled sharply, the thought hitting him like a punch to the gut. It wasn't just about marriage or kids—it was about being enough.

He thought of the treehouse, the throne they'd built together, the plaque honoring his mother. That project had been the first time in a long while he'd felt like himself—like the man Grace saw in him.

But was that enough?

The noise of the workshop seemed to close in around him, the weight of everything pressing down on his shoulders. Ethan pushed to his feet, needing air, space, something to clear his head.

He stepped outside, the cool evening breeze brushing against his face. The town square was quiet, the storefronts bathed in the soft glow of streetlights. He leaned against the brick wall of the workshop, staring up at the sky.

Somewhere in the distance, a train whistle blew, low and mournful. It reminded him of leaving Ashville all those years ago, of the promises he'd made to himself about the life he wanted to build.

He'd kept those promises. He'd built something good, something solid. But now, standing here, he wondered if he'd missed the point.

Maybe it wasn't just about building something for himself. Maybe it was about building something *with* someone else.

Ethan closed his eyes, the image of Grace flashing behind his lids—her laughter, her frustration, the way she looked at him like he was more than the sum of his mistakes.

He knew what he wanted. He'd always known.

The question was, did he have the courage to fight for it?

Ethan sat at the edge of his bed, the early morning sunlight casting long shadows across the room. His hands rested on his knees, head bowed as if in prayer, though his thoughts were far from peaceful. The hollow ache in his chest had grown louder, an undeniable signal that something had to change.

He thought back to the look in Grace's eyes the night before—a mixture of love and quiet resignation, as though she was holding onto him with every ounce of strength but knew her grip was slipping. He had spent too many nights drowning in schedules, contracts, and numbers, convincing himself it was for their future, all while neglecting the very reason he wanted a future at all.

The echoes of his father's voice, gruff and dismissive, whispered in his mind. *Work is everything. You have to be a provider—nothing else matters.* Ethan clenched his fists. He had vowed not to become that man, yet here he was, slipping into the same pattern.

Taking a deep breath, Ethan rose and grabbed his phone. He scrolled through his contacts and started sending messages to his team. "Effective immediately, I'm restructuring my schedule. You're all more than capable of handling the day-to-day operations. Let's talk at the shop later this week."

For the first time in months, Ethan felt a flicker of relief. He could trust his team. He had trained them well, and the business would survive.

That afternoon, Ethan found himself standing in front of the town's small jewelry store. His heart pounded as he stepped inside, the little bell above the door announcing his arrival.

"Afternoon, Mr. Blackwell," the jeweler greeted warmly. "What can I help you with?"

Ethan hesitated, his fingers brushing over the smooth wood of the counter. He smiled faintly. "I'm looking for an engagement ring."

The jeweler's face lit up. "Well, congratulations! Any particular style in mind?"

Ethan thought for a moment, his mind drifting to Grace. He pictured her hands—strong yet delicate, often smudged with pencil marks from her sketches or sawdust from the workshop. She didn't care for flashy things. She valued meaning over extravagance.

"Something simple," Ethan said. "Elegant, timeless. It has to feel like her—graceful."

The jeweler nodded knowingly and began pulling out a tray of rings. Ethan's eyes settled on a gold band with a single, sparkling diamond nestled in a modest setting. It was perfect—unassuming yet radiant, much like Grace herself.

"This one," he said without hesitation.

Later that evening, Ethan arrived home with the ring tucked safely in his pocket. The house felt warmer somehow, as if his resolve to put Grace first had already started to breathe life into the walls. He found her in the kitchen, humming softly as she prepared dinner.

He stepped closer, wrapping his arms around her waist from behind. She jumped slightly at his touch but then relaxed, leaning into him.

"You're home early," she said with a hint of surprise.

"I'm going to be home early every night," Ethan replied, his voice steady.

She turned in his arms, her brow furrowed. "What do you mean?"

"I mean I'm done putting work before us," he said, cupping her face in his hands. "I've been so afraid of turning into my father that I've been blind to the fact that I was heading down the same road. I don't want that life, Grace. I don't want to lose you."

Her eyes softened, tears threatening to spill. "Ethan…"

He pressed his forehead to hers. "I'm going to make this right. I promise. Starting with this."

He reached into his pocket, his heart pounding, and pulled out the small velvet box. Grace gasped, her hands flying to her mouth as he dropped to one knee.

"Grace," he began, his voice trembling. "I don't have all the answers, but I know this—I want to build a life with you. Not just a house or a business, but a life full of love and partnership. Will you marry me?"

Tears streamed down her cheeks as she nodded, her voice barely a whisper. "Yes, Ethan. A thousand times, yes."

As he slipped the ring onto her finger, Ethan felt a weight lift from his shoulders. For the first time in years, he knew he was exactly where he was meant to be.

Ethan stood at the head of the long conference table in the workshop's office, his hands resting on the polished wood surface. The hum of chatter among his team quieted as the clock struck the hour. They looked at him with a mix of curiosity and respect, each of them seated with notebooks and tablets at the ready.

Clearing his throat, Ethan began, "I want to thank all of you for taking the time to meet today. This isn't your typical status update meeting. It's about something more important—how we move forward as a team."

His employees exchanged glances, a hint of tension filling the room. Grace, seated to his right, gave him an encouraging nod.

"For years," Ethan continued, "I've been driven by one thing: building this business from the ground up. I poured everything I had into it because it gave me purpose, and it gave me hope when I didn't think I had any left. But in doing that, I've lost sight of something equally important—balance."

He took a breath, letting the weight of his words sink in.

"I've realized that I can't keep running this business the way I have been without sacrificing things that matter more to me. So, I'm making a change. From now on, I'll be scaling back my hours."

A murmur rippled through the room. Ethan held up a hand to silence it gently.

"Don't misunderstand me," he said firmly. "I'm not stepping away. Grace and I will still be here to guide you, to help with designs, and to tackle challenges when they arise. But I'm entrusting each of you to take the lead on projects, to use the skills you've developed, and to meet the high standards this business has always stood for. I trust all of you."

One of the senior woodworkers, Nate, leaned forward. "Ethan, we'll do our best, but…are you sure about this? You've been the backbone of this place since day one."

Ethan smiled. "And now it's time for the rest of you to carry it forward. You've all shown me that you're more than capable. The quality of your work speaks for itself, and I've never been prouder of a team than I am of this one. I've built a foundation here, and now it's time for all of us to build on it together."

Grace chimed in, her voice steady and warm. "We're not going anywhere. But we also believe that for this business to thrive, it can't rely solely on one person. You're all part of this legacy, and we know you'll keep it going strong."

The room grew quiet again, this time with a different energy—determination and unity.

Nate nodded. "You've got it, boss. We'll hold it down."

Another voice piped up from the back, "Yeah, we've got this. You've taught us well."

Ethan's chest swelled with gratitude. "Thank you, all of you. This isn't just a business to me—it's a family. And I'm counting on this family to help me find the balance I need."

As the meeting concluded, Ethan lingered, shaking hands and sharing quiet words of encouragement with each team member. When the room finally emptied, Grace approached him, a small smile on her lips.

"Well," she said, "how does it feel to let go a little?"

Ethan exhaled, the tension he hadn't realized he was carrying finally releasing. "It feels terrifying," he admitted. "But it also feels right."

Grace slipped her hand into his. "It is right, Ethan. And you're not letting go—you're making room for something bigger. For us."

He squeezed her hand, the weight of the moment settling into something lighter, something hopeful. Together, they walked out of the office, ready to embrace the next chapter.

Chapter Twelve

The morning sun peeked through the curtains, casting a soft, golden glow across the room. Grace stood before the mirror, her hands trembling slightly as she adjusted the delicate lace of her wedding dress. The gown had been chosen together, carefully selected to reflect the new chapter they were about to begin. She had never imagined a day like this—never imagined a man like Ethan Blackwell would stand by her side, his promises no longer uncertain but carved into the very foundation of their lives.

Behind her, the bustle of the wedding preparations could still be heard, but for a moment, everything was still. She took in a deep breath, trying to steady her heart, but there was no holding back the excitement or the fear that tugged at her chest. This was the culmination of everything they had fought for, of every moment they had shared. It was real now—so real it made her knees weak.

Ethan was downstairs, pacing around, no doubt running over his speech one last time. They hadn't planned a huge ceremony, but what they had planned was intimate, with a small gathering of friends and family, and the people who mattered most to them—Maria, Joe, and the team that had supported them through it all.

"Are you ready, love?" Grace's mother's voice cut through the moment. Her reflection smiled warmly, her eyes glistening with pride.

"I think I am," Grace whispered, turning to face her.

Her mother reached out, smoothing a stray strand of hair behind Grace's ear. "You're beautiful, sweetie. Just remember that you don't have to rush through today. It's yours. Every moment of it."

Grace nodded, feeling the tears threatening to spill over. She hadn't expected the rush of emotion this morning, hadn't expected it to hit so hard. The road to this day had been long and complicated, but she had Ethan by her side, and that made everything feel like it was falling into place.

Downstairs, Ethan was pacing by the window, hands shoved into the pockets of his suit, a far cry from the man he had been when he first arrived in Ashville. The past few months had been full of growth—of taking risks and learning to trust, of facing his fears and choosing to love. He looked out across the yard, where the same oak tree stood, the one that had once been the backdrop to his childhood dreams, and now, it was the symbol of something new, something lasting.

Maria had been right. He wasn't his father. He wasn't that man.

It was a realization that came to him on the drive here, when everything he had built, everything he had worked for, finally came together. He knew what mattered now. What he had with Grace—this love, this life—was everything.

As the minutes ticked by, the knot in his stomach tightened, but it wasn't from fear anymore. It was excitement. It was the realization that he was no longer holding back.

He looked up as Grace entered the room, her face flushed, eyes sparkling with a mix of nerves and joy. She was breathtaking, the very image of everything he had ever wanted, standing before him in that gown, like a dream he never dared to let himself have.

"You look…" He swallowed, his voice cracking for a moment. "You look incredible."

Grace smiled softly, walking toward him, her steps slow, deliberate. She reached out to him, her fingers brushing his chest.

"I think we're ready, Ethan," she said, her voice barely a whisper, but the weight of her words landed with all the importance of the vows they were about to make.

He took her hand, holding it in his, the warmth of her palm seeping into his own. "You've always been ready," he said, his voice steady now, filled with certainty. "I'm just glad you're here with me."

As they stood there together, the door to the outside world opened, and the guests began to arrive. Their friends and family gathered in the small clearing by the treehouse, which had been transformed for the occasion. The branches above them were decorated with strands of fairy lights, glistening like stars, and soft flowers lined the edges of the space.

The ceremony was short but meaningful, every word spoken with love and conviction. The vows they exchanged were simple, but they carried all the weight of everything they had overcome, everything they had learned about each other and themselves. Ethan promised to always fight for them, to always trust in their future together. Grace promised to stand by him, to build a life with him, no matter the challenges that lay ahead.

The kiss that sealed their vows was tender, the promise of forever lingering in the air, as their friends and family cheered, the sound of joy echoing through the trees.

For the first time in years, Ethan felt the weight of his past lift entirely, replaced with something new—a future that was his to build, one day at a time, with the woman he loved at his side.

As the reception began, the laughter and warmth surrounding them was everything Ethan had dreamed of when he first stepped into Ashville all those months ago. But now, it was his life, his home, and with Grace beside him, he knew nothing would ever pull them apart again.

This was where he was meant to be.

This was his beginning.

A Year Later

The soft hum of a brush sliding against the wall filled the room, the scent of fresh paint lingering in the air. Ethan stepped back, his hand resting on his hip as he surveyed the pale green hue they'd chosen for the nursery. The color reminded him of spring mornings, full of life and hope, perfect for the tiny new member of their family set to arrive in just a few short months.

Behind him, Grace stood with a paintbrush in hand, her movements deliberate as she focused on the trim near the window. Her baby bump was prominent now, and Ethan couldn't help but glance over his shoulder at her, his heart swelling at the sight.

"Careful, Grace," he said, setting his brush down and moving closer. "You've been at it for hours. You should take a break."

Grace laughed softly, her free hand resting on her belly. "I'm fine, Ethan. I'm pregnant, not fragile."

"Still," he insisted, taking the brush from her and setting it on the tray. "I don't want you overdoing it."

She rolled her eyes but let him guide her to the rocking chair they'd brought up earlier. It had been his mother's chair, lovingly restored and polished, now ready for its next chapter in their growing family. Grace eased into it with a sigh, her fingers absently tracing the carved arms.

"You know," she said, a teasing smile playing on her lips, "if you're this overprotective now, I can't imagine what you'll be like when the baby gets here."

Ethan chuckled, kneeling in front of her and resting his hands on her knees. "Probably insufferable. You'll have to rein me in."

She brushed her fingers through his hair, her eyes softening. "You're going to be an amazing dad, Ethan."

Her words struck something deep in him, a mix of joy and trepidation. He wanted to believe her, and maybe he was starting to. Over the past year, he'd worked hard to move past the shadow of his father's legacy, to build a life filled with love and intention. Grace had been there every step of the way, her unwavering support pulling him through even his darkest moments.

"I just…" he started, his voice faltering slightly. "I don't want to mess this up."

Grace tilted her head, her expression serious but kind. "You won't. You've already made this house a home, a real one. You've shown me every day how much you care, not just about me, but about this family we're building. That's what matters."

Ethan nodded, leaning forward to rest his forehead against hers. "You always know what to say, don't you?"

"Someone has to keep you in line," she teased, her smile returning.

He stood and stretched, glancing around the room. The nursery was starting to come together—the walls painted, shelves installed, and the beginnings of a mural on one side. On the floor near the window sat the beginnings of the crib, the pieces carefully cut and sanded, waiting to be assembled.

"Ready to help me with the crib?" he asked, holding out his hand.

Grace took it, letting him pull her to her feet. "I thought you'd never ask."

Together, they moved to the crib parts, Grace holding the pieces steady as Ethan secured them in place. They worked quietly for a while, their movements synchronized, the occasional laugh or teasing comment breaking the silence. It felt natural, the way they complemented each other, the way they tackled every project as a team.

As they tightened the final screw, Grace sat back on her heels, admiring their work. "It's perfect," she said softly, her hand resting on her belly.

Ethan reached over, placing his hand over hers. "No," he said, his voice low and full of emotion. "This is perfect."

They stayed like that for a moment, the weight of what they were building together settling around them. Grace leaned against his shoulder, her eyes drifting to the small bookshelf Ethan had made earlier in the year, now filled with children's books they'd picked out together.

"I sold my house today," she said suddenly, breaking the silence.

Ethan turned to her, his eyebrows lifting in surprise. "You did?"

She nodded. "It's time. This is our home now. It feels right."

His heart swelled at her words, a sense of completion washing over him. The house, once a place of pain and regret, had become a symbol of everything he'd hoped for—family, love, and a future worth fighting for.

"Thank you," he said simply, his voice thick with emotion.

Grace smiled, her eyes shining. "You don't have to thank me, Ethan. This is where I want to be. With you."

As the sun began to set, casting a warm glow across the room, they stood together in the nursery, the promise of their future stretching out before them. For the first time in a long time, Ethan felt completely at peace.

Ethan pushed open the heavy door of the workshop, the familiar scent of sawdust and varnish greeting him like an old friend. Inside, the place hummed with activity. The rhythmic buzz of saws, the sharp clatter of tools, and the low murmur of voices blended into a symphony of productivity.

He paused near the entrance, taking in the sight. Ben, one of his newer employees, was carefully measuring and cutting a large piece of oak while Jess, a designer Grace had personally trained, was sketching plans for a custom dining set. Ethan smiled. It felt good to see the place thriving, even in his occasional absence.

"Hey, boss!" Ben called out, lifting a hand in greeting.

"Morning, Ben," Ethan replied, stepping further into the workshop. "How's that table coming along?"

Ben grinned, brushing sawdust off his shirt. "Coming together nicely. Should be ready for assembly by tomorrow. Jess's design is a little tricky, but I think we've got it figured out."

Ethan glanced over at the plans Jess was working on, nodding in approval. "Looks like a challenge, but I have no doubt you'll pull it off. You always do."

Jess looked up from her sketchbook, a smirk on her face. "Flattery won't get you out of reviewing the finished product, Ethan. You're still the final say, remember?"

He chuckled, holding up his hands. "Wouldn't dream of dodging my responsibilities."

Moving through the workshop, Ethan checked in with each team member, offering advice when needed and words of encouragement where he could. It wasn't long before he made his way to the back, where Adam, one of his apprentices, was sanding a chair.

"Adam," Ethan said, crouching down to inspect the work. "How's it coming along?"

Adam looked up, a nervous smile on his face. "I think it's good, but I can't get the edges as smooth as I want them."

Ethan nodded, running his fingers along the curve of the wood. "It's solid work, but I see what you mean. Let me show you a trick."

Grabbing a piece of sandpaper, Ethan demonstrated a subtle technique, carefully guiding Adam through the process. "It's all in the pressure and the angle," he explained. "Too much force, and you'll take off more than you want. Too little, and it'll take forever. Find the balance."

Adam mimicked the motion, his hands steadying as he worked. After a few tries, he looked up, his face lighting up with pride. "That's it! Thanks, Ethan."

Ethan clapped him on the shoulder. "You're getting there. Keep at it."

As he straightened, Ethan caught sight of Grace entering the workshop, her presence immediately drawing his attention. She carried a box of pastries from the local bakery, her smile bright as she approached the group.

"Thought you all could use a pick-me-up," she said, setting the box on a workbench.

The team swarmed the treats, offering their thanks as Grace sidled up to Ethan. "Everything running smoothly?" she asked, her gaze sweeping the room.

"Better than I expected," Ethan admitted. "They've really stepped up. I might just be able to take that paternity leave you keep talking about."

Grace arched an eyebrow, her smile turning teasing. "You mean the one I've been demanding you take?"

He laughed, leaning down to kiss her cheek. "Exactly."

The sight of his employees working with such dedication, of Grace standing beside him with her unwavering support, filled Ethan with a deep sense of gratitude. The workshop wasn't just a business—it was a testament to how far he'd come and how much he had to look forward to.

As the morning wore on, Ethan lingered, helping where needed and offering guidance. The team was competent and passionate, and for the first time in a long time, he felt confident that the workshop could thrive without his constant oversight.

And that, he realized, was a gift—not just for him, but for the family he was building with Grace.

Seven Years Later

The late afternoon sun bathed the front yard in a warm, golden glow. Laughter and the hum of conversation filled the air as employees, friends, and family gathered to celebrate Ethan's early retirement. Long tables draped in white linen stood under the shade of the massive oak tree, laden with platters of food and pitchers of lemonade. Twinkling lights were strung from the branches, promising a magical ambiance once night fell.

Ethan stood with Grace near the tree, his hand resting lightly on her back. The years had been kind to them. The fine lines at the corners of their eyes spoke of countless smiles and shared laughter. Ethan's hair was speckled with gray, and Grace's face held a calm, settled happiness that only deep love and contentment could bring.

"Can you believe this?" Ethan asked, gesturing toward the bustling scene. "I never thought this day would come."

Grace leaned into him, her smile soft. "You've earned it, Ethan. It's time for you to enjoy everything you've built—for us, for this family."

Lilly approached them with a confident stride, her clipboard tucked under her arm. She had been Grace's right-hand designer and had quickly risen to become one of the most reliable and respected members of their team. Her brown hair was pulled into a neat bun, and her sharp eyes scanned the crowd, ensuring everything was running smoothly.

"Boss—well, former boss," Lilly corrected herself with a grin, "everything's set. Contracts are lined up for the next quarter, and the team is ready for the transition. I won't let you down."

Ethan smiled, pride shining in his eyes. "I know you won't, Lilly. I couldn't ask for a better person to take the reins. You've got this."

Lilly looked to Grace, who nodded in agreement. "You've been with us since the beginning, Lilly. There's no one we trust more to take over."

Lilly's smile faltered briefly as emotion flickered across her face. "Thank you, both of you. This place isn't just a job; it's a family. I'll take care of it like it's my own."

Before anyone could respond, a small, excited voice called out from above.

"Daddy! Mommy! Look!"

All heads turned toward the treehouse, perched high in the oak tree, now restored to its former glory and then some. A little girl, no more than six, peeked out from the window, her bright green eyes and wavy chestnut hair a perfect blend of her parents. She waved enthusiastically, clutching a stuffed rabbit in her free hand.

"Clara!" Ethan called up, laughing. "Be careful, sweetheart."

"She's fine," Grace assured him with a chuckle. "It's her kingdom, after all."

Clara leaned further out the window, grinning. "I'm the queen now, Daddy!"

Ethan pressed a hand to his chest, mockingly pretending to faint. "The queen has spoken. I'm officially retired."

The crowd laughed, and Clara giggled, pulling back into the treehouse to resume her play.

As the party continued, Ethan found himself taking a moment to soak it all in. The workshop had grown into a thriving business, their employees were more like family, and he and Grace had built a life filled with love and purpose.

He wrapped an arm around Grace, drawing her close. "Thank you for pushing me, for believing in me, for being my everything."

She smiled up at him, her eyes glistening. "I always knew this was where we'd end up, Ethan. Together, where we belong."

The evening settled into a contented rhythm, laughter and joy filling the air as the lights in the tree twinkled against the deepening twilight. Ethan knew that the threads of fate had led him exactly where he was meant to be, and there was no greater gift than that.

The End...

Life has a way of pulling us in directions we never expected, weaving threads of joy, pain, loss, and hope into a tapestry that is uniquely ours. Like Ethan, we often fear the shadows of our past, letting them hold us back from embracing the present or dreaming of a better future. But life isn't about perfection—it's about growth. It's about finding the courage to let go of what was, to fight for what is, and to believe in what could be.

Love, like life, is messy and unpredictable, but it's also the most beautiful thread of all. It reminds us that we're never truly alone, that the people we meet along the way can shape us, heal us, and lead us home.

So, as you turn this final page, may you find the strength to mend the threads of your own life, to face the unknown with courage, and to cherish the people who walk beside you. Because no matter where you've been or what you've lost, the threads of fate have a way of leading you exactly where you're meant to be.

Life is a journey, and the threads of fate weave paths that surprise us all. Through joy, pain, and love, we grow and learn to embrace who we're meant to be. Ethan and Grace's story reminds us that it's never too late to follow your heart and find your way home.

But this is just one story among many. Every thread connects to another, and every life holds a tale worth telling. Keep an eye out for the next chapters in the *Threads of Fate* series—stories of love, resilience, and the courage it takes to rewrite destiny.

Thank you for joining me on this journey. I hope these stories inspire you to mend the threads of your own life and to hold tight to the connections that matter most.

~ Evelyn Cross

Printed in Great Britain
by Amazon